THE HEAT OF OTHERS

A novel by Morgane Billuart

This work is dedicated to Juli

from: ghanerarphard@gmail.com
to: maxkeller@gmail.com
object: Problematics and Possibilities of Mind-Enhancement Final Selection List

Dear Max Keller,

We are delighted to inform you that you have been selected to participate in the 2028 Conference *Beyond the Given Mind: Possibilities and Dilemmas of Enhancement*. The selection process was highly competitive and rigorous, but your application distinguished itself through your exemplary reference letters and esteemed publications.

Please find attached a Non-Disclosure Agreement that we kindly ask you to review, sign, and return before your arrival. Additionally, your flight tickets to Svalbard and other important information are included for your convenience.

We look forward to welcoming you next week and engaging with your insights at the conference.

Best regards,

Ghaner Arphard and Jorly Benton

1.

At the airport security gates, Max positioned her belongings in the box on the conveyor belt, carefully removing each of her rings and her necklace. One by one, the delicate pieces were laid out.

As she passed through the body check, a young man standing at the checkpoint asked her to turn right. Max approached him, smiling awkwardly, unsure of her crime. After glancing at her slim waist and then staring into her grey irises, his gaze transfigured. He flashed his hand into her bag, gazing at Max with policing eyes, finally pulling out the small but sharp knife. Max, half-honest, feigned astonishment and apologized, pretending to have forgotten about the airport rules and the presence of the not-so-innocent blade.

The man stared back, stood still for a moment and, instead of putting it away, discreetly slipped the weapon back into the bag. He closed it silently and handed it back to Max, adding a slight nod.

Just for today, she would get away with it.
She thought of all the equipped women who had crossed the threshold of an airport, dangerously passing through portals.

***

As the flight attendant was passing by, she ordered a glass of wine and swallowed her first Xanax. Taking her first sips, she glanced at her neighbor's choice of film: a climate dystopia. As the plane departed, Max saw the disastrous scenes on the screen unfold from the corner of her eye. Not yet sedated, she swallowed her anxiety again and again, but every small turbulence felt like the sharpest reminder of life's delicateness.

She breathed slowly, settling back into the narrow seat and agonizing, as usual, whether this flight might be her last.

On her neighbor's screen, the climate catastrophe continued, relentless and horrifying. Finally, Max drifted into a light sleep, cradled by the fragile calm the pills had given her.

Yet, before long, the plane's jolting movements roused her, and her trembling, too-wet palm snatched her neighbor's unfamiliar hand.

"I'm sorry," Max gasped.

Speaking about life after the flight, the stranger attempted to distract Max, uttering mantras that assured her of a life beyond the plane's carcass: "Svalbard? That is... great! You're going to have an amazing time. A wonderful one... I'm sure about that."

Max faintly grimaced, squeezing her eyes at every small jolt, tightening her grip ever more on the young man's hand.

When the plane finally landed in Oslo, Max released her breath; her hand was soaked in her neighbour's palm. She pulled it out, wiped it against her sweater, thanked him, grabbed her suitcase, and left.

She was greeted by a twilight scene of snow-covered cars and transport agents, their movement hindered by the accumulation of falling flurries. An icy wind met the lingering sweat and jolted her awake: she had survived the flight! Her skin was kissed by Norway's freezing breeze, and every breath passed through her throat like crushed ice.

She scanned the specs attached to the email, which specified that she should wait patiently until 4:30 PM for the next plane to depart for Longyearbyen Airport. Sitting down at the indicated terminal, Max looked at the endless walls of glass, contemplating the sea of darkness surrounding her.

Suddenly, a foreign hand clutched her shoulder.

Max propelled into alertness.

"Are you going to the conference?"

Max turned around.

"Embarkation has already begun," the young man said. "It'd be a shame to miss the flight."

Still slightly numb from the Xanax, Max loosely got a hold of her bag and walked toward the gate. In silence, she and the man scanned their tickets, entered the sealed corridor, and wandered toward the small plane.

Max was haunted by the thought of another ride. Although many seats remained unoccupied, the stranger sat next to her, naturally.

"Where are you flying from?"

"Vienna. You?"

"Munich."

"You sound American."

"I studied in the US."

Max remained quiet.

Triggered by her placidity, he continued: "What do you do?"

"I'm a researcher. Media theory."

Max said nothing more.

"I'm a biotechnologist."

She glanced at the young man, as though he had uttered something that piqued her interest.

"What's your specialty?"

"Biotechnology and ethics. Regulatory and social aspects of biotech."

"Nice," muttered Max as she finished the last sip from her water bottle.

The pilot began announcing a few details about the trajectory, along with potential turbulence due to stormy, snow-laden winds.

The last flight. It's the last flight, Max told herself, trying to calm down while recalling the gentle memory of being carried in her parents' car. Then, the shaking of the engine had not mattered as the body was reassured by the ambient heat of the machine.

This time, Max tried to avoid looking at her neighbor's activities, keeping her eyes fixed on the flight information display.

"By the way, I'm Amos."

"Damos, cool."

"No, I said Amos."

"Sorry," answered Max, "I'm terrible with names."

"You're Max, right?" answered Amos with an unsettling grin. "I saw your name on the event's program."

Max nodded and fixated her gaze back on the screen.

On the map, the plane remained at its initial position, as if frozen in time. Surely it was flying, shaking in every direction, yet its path on the screen resembled an endless journey caught between the present and the past. Gripped by panic at the thought of an engine malfunction, Max swung around to face the stranger again: "So, bioethics... Tell me more?"

"What do you want to know?"

"Well... is the body an obstacle to technology?" asked Max, ironically smirking.

"Touché," replied Amos, "I guess I'm the wrong person to ask. Any treatment or form of technology can be considered as progress or enhancement. Sometimes the body does not react well, but it does not mean that it is not good for the human race and its development."

"The human race..." Max rolled her eyes.

"Not the answer you expected?" weighed Amos.

"For a conference on possibilities and casualties, you already seem to have picked a side," retorted Max.

"What would we all discuss if we all already agreed?"

Max pretended to look for something on the menu. Still, from the corner of her eye, she could feel the curiosity and gaze of the man sitting at her side. Softly, Amos took a book out of his bag. The title, *Rewriting Life: The New Frontiers of Bioengineering,* appeared in bold letters over an icy blue landscape.

Max stared at the relic for a while.

"Seeking to live forever, ah?" asked Max with a confrontational smile.

Amos paused, his gaze tracing Max's body.

"How old are you?" he asked.

"Twenty-eight"

"Yeah," Amos whispered. "You can still afford not to

think about that."

When Max lurked outside the window, the plane seemed to have entered another universe. The sky had become darker. There was no light nor a shadow of a horizon to be seen. With the weight of her head against the window, unsure if Amos would even hear her, she mumbled: "Is life *that great*?"

There was no reply.

2.

As the plane landed, Max looked out of the window, but there was nothing for her gaze to rest on. Svalbard resembled an ocean of infinite shadows with rare sparkles of life. Only the few beams illuminating the path to the Science Center guided her eyes.

After disembarking from the plane, a long black shuttle carried them, along with the other guests, to the facility. Nearing its destination, Max noticed what looked like the carcass of a machine, resembling a strange hybrid creature. Squinting at the scenery, she saw that the building was strangely adorned with numerous connecting pipes that seemed to come and go from all sides. Against the dark, migratory horizon of the Svalbard landscape, the Science Center stood out like a poor animal encumbered by trials, like a child born too early, a brain that couldn't function without pipes.

"What the fuck is that?" whispered Amos, staring at the faint clues in the darkness.

Max slowly discerned the shapes and forms of countless ventilation pipelines running along the once minimalist and elegant Science Center, a monument she had only seen in pictures. The white and grey tubes were covering the entire structure, transforming it into a sad, somewhat enchained creature.

As she exited the car, a gust of cold air and icy wind caught her off guard. She paused to catch her breath.

Guided by the directions of the man who picked them up, Amos was already striding ahead with his suitcases toward what looked like an airlock.

He looked back.

"Do you want me to take your luggage?"

Max's eyes alone dismissed the offer.

After a chain of beeps and unlocking doors, the group crossed the airlock and finally entered the building. Max was surprised to find a warm, wooden interior that seemed to thaw her from within. The walls of the Center, coated in beige and orange hues, transfigured its hostile exterior impression into an unexpectedly inviting belly. Far from a decaying or dying body, the space evoked the old promises of arrival and reaching a destination after a long winter's drive.

The warmth and brightness spread throughout the main entrance, where a dozen strangers had gathered around elegant hostesses handing out keys and giving directions. Max got hers, unsure yet of the building's floorplan. She looked at the leaflet. It indicated that the elevators on the right led to the dorms, where she had to find room number thirteen.

She rushed that way.

As the doors of the elevator opened, Max encountered a long, orange, and somewhat damp corridor with a wooden floor softly squeaking at every step.

Finally having reached her room, she collapsed onto the floor, savoring the sensation of something steady and warm to hold her back. No more shakes, no more turbulence.

Lying on her back, Max looked around. The space offered no more than a desk, a bathroom, and a single bed. The muffled carpet, which she had sunk into, reminded her of seventies interiors, inhabited by the smells of a grandfather who had passed.

Max decided to get up and began unpacking her suitcase, placing her few pieces of clothes and skincare products in their designated spots.

The only object left was the knife.

She grabbed it and tucked it beneath the mattress, just under the bedframe, positioning it carefully in the bottom-left corner and making sure it remained out of reach. Sitting down in the room's only chair, Max noticed a leaflet on the table outlining the event and its full agenda.

The mandatory tour was scheduled to begin soon. She ran out.

***

At the entrance, a group of visitors appeared puzzled and unsure of which space they had arrived in.

From one corner, a man appeared, followed by a younger one who had already begun filming him. His voice, tinged with an accent Max had never heard before, announced: "We're expecting more people... but as it seems, some guests and speakers haven't yet arrived. For security and timely reasons, I'll go ahead with the tour and start right now."

As the crowd moved into the body of the main floor, Max crept forward, studying the artifacts and tools embedded in the walls and beams. Curious and almost prosthetic, they seemed to serve as both support and decoration, imbuing the space with a dangerously intriguing aura. In a strangely fitting way, they merged with the rest of the scene: the eerie building, the dark landscape, the endless cold, and the palette of warmth and life.

"The Science Center," the guide cheered, "has served for decades as a central hub for Arctic scientific research. It boasts state-of-the-art laboratories, renowned scientists, and countless accolades to its name."

With pride, the guide continued, reciting an endless list of names and events on their agenda. "This facility not only serves as a beacon of education and research, but also stands as a testament to human ingenuity amid the challenges of such an environment."

Tuning into the guide's voice, the group continued their uncanny ascent and descent around the building. Every wall, covered in wood, was adorned with intricate, almost mechanical designs that seemed to pulse with a life of their own. In every possible corner, pipelines and cables were softly coming up to the surface, like veins under a foundation that softly fades out.

"You have probably noticed the pipelines going in and out of this house. Our prided space has been redesigned and shaped according to the vision of the renowned architect Paul Nachman, aiming to push the limits of climate and energy transfer, creating a building in which human heat can be harvested and redistributed over time."

"Circular energy? Ironic how they've flown us all in for

a whole week and still praise for this kind of design," a stranger whispered.

Another guest, glancing around with a wry smile, added: "Would you have preferred if they held the entire conference on a ferry, perhaps?"

Max walked slowly, fascinated by the strangeness and hybridity of the two opposing forces that collided: the cold silver against the warmth, the dimmed life against the dark.

The final space they entered was, on the contrary, conventional. The meeting room contained only a round table, shaped like an infinite loop with negative space in the center, and chairs neatly aligned. The blue projection on the screen displayed a smooth light, contrasting with the warm yellow tones of the ambience: a promising, generous atmosphere that felt vibrant rather than sterile.

The guide continued: "This is the room where most conversations and debates will unfold. It's free to use, but there are pre-arranged, scheduled moments when the entire cohort should gather. The first meeting is set in three days to clarify the needs and key aspects of the event. This is also where the writing of the final report will take place."

Having reached the end of his introduction, the guide steered the small crowd back toward the entrance and said: "As you may consider, constructing a building and operating an enterprise in such a hostile environment requires strict adherence to certain rules. The first one is that no windows can be opened. This is to maintain efficient heat redistribution. Additionally, every door and space must be carefully closed, and outside excursions or exit doors should be opened and closed with the utmost attention."

He then turned around and asked the young man to stop filming.

"Now, if you ever want to walk outside of this space, which I'm sure you will, there are a few more things you should be aware of."

Max slowly looked around, only to discover the intrigued faces of the other guests and lecturers.

"Walking around the perimeters is dangerous, and you might encounter species that do not want you around. Unlike many parts of Europe where firearms are rarely seen outside of specialized contexts, here in polar bear country, the situation is... quite different."

He paused.

"With around 5,000 firearms for nearly 2,500 residents, Longyearbyen boasts a weapon density that rivals even the famed Texan standards."

The crowd remained silent.

"In Longyearbyen, what was once a straightforward process of obtaining a heavy-caliber firearm with just an ID has become more difficult. Now, renting a firearm requires proof of legal entitlement, such as a European firearms pass or a valid hunting license."

An air of suspicion swept through the crowd, each person eyeing the others with wary glances.

The guide broke the tension, his voice cutting through the uneasy silence: "To clear things up and ensure we're all on the same page, could those with a gun license please raise their hands?"

Amos slowly raised his, as if ashamed.

The rest of the crowd fixated on him, analyzing the status of the key holder of a power no one yet knew the extent of.

"For everyone else, please schedule any excursions and

outside meetings with Ilo, our technical assistant."

The guide pointed to a calm figure standing in the corner of the room.

"Ilo holds a license and will be available to escort you if you ever need to go outside," he added. "Make sure to contact her in advance with any requests, as we also need her on site for technical issues related to the building and other matters of that kind."

Max stared at Ilo, struck by a sense of discovery.

She was the epitome of androgyny, a striking blend of features that defied conventional definitions. Her gently curved yet strong features were a perfect mix of softness and strength. Taller than average, her demeanor resembled that of a dancer, with her head held straight and poised. Her hands appeared strong and well-crafted, reflecting the many skills she had probably accumulated over the years. Her long, thick black hair, styled in two buns, suggested a fertile, almost optimal nature.

Max observed her affectionately.

It was both strange and oddly fitting that this enigmatic figure could be the key to escaping such a building.

She etched Ilo's face into her memory, somewhat determined to get closer to one of those who held the key to the outside world.

After finishing his speech, the guide rushed around the room distributing badges and necklaces showcasing everyone's accreditations.

With a light chuckle, he remarked, "Well, as you may know, this isn't a big town. However, if you find yourself stirring things up on the island or if any locals question your presence, just show them this card."

Then, he announced that the first dinner would be served in the small amphitheater, warmly inviting all the guests to follow him.

***

Stepping into the spacious and elegant room, Max observed with unease the attentive hosts and hostesses stationed throughout. Unsure of whom to approach, she picked a random seat, her gaze falling onto the plates already set with meals and menus attached.

As she looked up, an unfamiliar face nearby offered her a friendly smile and an extended hand.

"Jona."

"I'm Max."

"We have a problem here."

"Excuse me?"

"They forgot about my allergies."

Max scanned the offerings.

Jona pointed at the gravlaks and lutefisk.

Max tilted her head.

Jona sighed and looked around the room, attempting to spot a hostess nearby.

"I'll be back."

As Max watched Jona walking away, her gaze fell upon Ilo, who had just entered the room. Captivated, Max couldn't help but marvel at her unique appearance. How could nature render such an enigmatic figure? In the dimly lit dinner room, Ilo's tanned skin accentuated the amber almond shape of her eyes, giving her a feline allure as if always poised to play or pounce. Her demeanor defied categorization as either ethereal or earthly; she embodied a perfect blend of femininity and masculinity, earth and sky. Max hesitated to stand up and reach out, but before she had the chance to, an older man intercepted Ilo by the arm, whispering something that made her retreat backward.

***

Strolling through the hallways in the direction of her room, Max noticed a low, persistent hum emanating from the pipelines. The sound wove itself into the building's background noise. It was a gentle and caring hum. Max followed the sound, wondering where it came from. The visions of the unchained building, sitting in an ocean of dimmed lights, did not leave her mind. There was a strange dissonance and almost absurd quality of experimenting with endless cables and pipelines in the middle of nature's jewels. The location was beautiful, surely, but did they truly have to travel that far?

There, at the end of the world, every step in the snow, every trace of human passage, every whiff of human presence seemed like nature's betrayal.

After all, thought Max, this wasn't the first time that great minds sought to represent themselves in the most reclusive, improbable, and memorable places. Such personas would never agree to meet in a godforsaken room somewhere in a suburban town, surrounded by pubs and overflowing garbage cans.

Back in her room, lying on the carpet, her head supported by the corner of the bed, Max stared at the ceiling while slowly caressing the floor. The soft carpet resembled a breathing animal, tender and warm.

She decided to get up, slowly moving toward the bathroom and starting to undress.

After washing her body and securely locking her door, Max settled in bed, caressed by the soft heat and the gentle hum of the distributed warmth. She reached under the mattress, her fingers searching until they brushed against the cold metal of the knife.

It was still there. Her twenty-fifth birthday gift. She was initially gifted a vintage pen, an old pen like no other, thick and heavy, probably suited to sign important files and contracts. Although polite, Max couldn't hide her disappointment at the sight of the present.

A few hours later, she and her oma were back at the shop where the pen was initially purchased, searching for an alternative tool, rummaging through heaps of knick-knacks and notebooks.

Looking up at the thousands of shelves within the store, Max's gaze met that of a simple and small knife, harmless but protruding.

"What for?" pondered her grandmother, eyeing her sceptically.

Max kept quiet, staring at the reflection of the object in its protected glass.

She clenched the object one more time before withdrawing her hand from beneath the matras. Alone and isolated in this small Norwegian cabinet, Max was finally locked in, safe from intrusions, shielded from any disturbances. In some way, she was stuck. Yet, the place resembled a shelter rather than a cage.

Nothing could touch or harm her this time.

Max closed her eyes, the building's voices lingering unsettlingly in her mind, engraving themselves with a strange persistence. The sounds, seemingly coming from the conduits, drifted from everywhere to nowhere like wires twisting into a knot. It was clear that alterations had been made to the building, modifications that the original architecture did not necessitate, changes that, if the structure could voice its opinion, it would have objected to.

Sitting amid Max's mind, the building morphed back into the strange, neglected being struggling to stay alive.

3.

At the start of each day, Max had taken the nasty, still religious habit of checking her work e-mail, as if any possible good news were about to arrive. Month after month, rejections came for proposals, jobs, and symposiums, keeping her in a quiet state of humility.

But at this point, and in this career path, denial wasn't an issue: it was the state of the art.

Luckily, on that first morning of the conference, there was no bad news, no deceiving emails, only the thrilling momentum of an event about to begin.

Max jumped out of bed and prepared quickly before heading to the main lounge.

When she finally entered the main hall for the opening lecture, twenty other individuals were already scattered throughout the expansive conference room. The vast space and its stage, all colored in soft blue and grey lights, swallowed the guests, making the gathering feel smaller and more intimate than it truly was. It was designed like a theater. The main speaking area featured not much more than a giant screen, a metal table, and two chairs.

Max envisioned a speaker walking in, the blue and greyish tones of the long curtains shimmering like pearls in the rain, rippling softly, enhancing the fluidity of their speech and movements.

She couldn't wait.

As more guests arrived, Max's personal choice of garments felt improper, too relaxed.

All the others were dressed in a curious, hybrid style that blended Silicon Valley chic with a corporate nonchalance.

With the soft heat settling in, they soon began to remove their layers, revealing the skin beneath. From her seat, Max recognized several faces she had encountered before, and a few she had only heard of. Confused and still struck by their physical presence, she stared at them with a mix of curiosity and disappointment, realizing that these intellectual giants were, after all, imperfect and quirky humans.

An old man positioned himself next to her, gently approaching her with an insistent smile. He gazed at Max without a word.

Deranged by his audacity, Max met his stare.

"Can I help you, perhaps?"

The old man stuttered as he invited Max to shake hands.

She observed his hand, responding with a forced smile. It was marked by time and life's unforeseen events, crowned with a wedding ring.

Max heard some whispering coming from the back of the room. Turning around, she noticed Ilo walking in her direction, handing her a piece of paper and a pen, adorned with a warm smile.

"What is this about?" Max asked, glancing at the document.

"Just another form about pictures, privacy, rights..."

"Are you also a speaker?"

"No. I make sure the building runs smoothly, or at least I try."

"I'm Max."

Ilo flashed a warm smile.

Max shyly mirrored the gesture before turning her gaze back to the platform. There, her sight fell onto two large cameras resembling fixed domes. One was aimed at the speakers, the other was scanning the crowd.

"What's up with the cameras?" Max asked.

"The majority of the event is recorded, and part of it will be publicly displayed."

Max raised an eyebrow.

"What did I sign an NDA for exactly?"

"Well," Ilo mused before replying, "even though the event will be public, some details might be edited out. There's always a backstage to every scene," she paused. "Don't you know that?"

Conversation slowly faded as a tiny, finely dressed woman appeared, her entrance drawing a tranquil silence that shortly erupted into applause. Ghaner Arphard walked on her side.

Max was caught off guard by his strange, enduring melancholy. There weren't many images of the philosopher online, but his physical envelope wasn't far from what she had imagined him to be. A distant, aloof figure, crystallized by the notion of a genius who never sees light: pale skin, curved shoulders, and smoky sunglasses shielding against anyone who would want to gaze into his eyes.

Max sat there, somewhat mesmerized. What had once been just a name on paper, a mere reference, was a living, breathing individual, no longer just a conceptual figure or a distant image.

The applause ceased suddenly, leaving only the faint hum of the building's ventilation system.

"Ladies and gentlemen, researchers and thinkers, technologists and designers, I have had no preparation for this opening speech... Except my entire life."

The crowd followed Ghaner's movements before bursting into applause again.

"Today, we gather here with a shared vision: to delve into the frontiers of mind-enhancement technologies, research, and practices, but most importantly, their possibilities and consequences. First and foremost, I would like to take this opportunity to thank the dear sponsor of such an event, Jorly Benton, for her undeniable presence and generous donation. We owe our presence today to your unwavering support."

The spectators turned toward the small, elegant, middle-aged lady, who returned their looks with a gesture of gratitude that still felt somehow habitual.

At fifty-two, though appearing ten years younger, Jorly Benton was no stranger to Max. Well known in research and philanthropy, she moved through both realms with an expertise that commanded respect. Yet, she had never created anything, nor did she write. Coming from a family that had harvested and collected industrial oil, Jorly had started focusing on spending her inheritance ethically, hoping somehow to contribute to a better world. Her patronage of think tanks and residencies devoted to technology and digital practices had made her a pivotal figure in that world.

At first and for many years after, she was known as the woman who organized one of the most exclusive parties in Los Angeles. The whole of Hollywood flocked there, attracted by the evening's reputation. Jorly had a knack for bringing together talents and intellects of all kinds, often sparking creative collaborations, through music and alcohol, that might never have seen the light of day elsewhere.

"Nothing's impossible," Jorly frequently cited, "If only you can connect the right minds." One day, she had put an end to the festivities.

Although interesting conversations and exchanges did happen during those eventful evenings, she had aged, and partying no longer fitted with her philanthropic ambitions. Now, she was fully set on restoring the family's reputation by contributing to numerous causes and remarkable projects.

"The idea is not to die rich," she would often say, repeating it like a cherished mantra.

If the outside world and the public eye were skeptical about whether such personas were in the best position at attempting to repair systems they had greatly contributed to destroying, Jorly disregarded the opinions of the masses.

She knew what money could afford.

"Technology, as we know it, is one of the many subtle weapons of the twenty-first century. But more dangerous than technology alone are the speculation, narratives, and science fiction undergoing their parade, making it more and more difficult for individuals to comprehend the real consequences of what many call 'technological progress'. I argue here that *the Digital Mundane* is what any ethicist, designer, or philosopher should be concerned with. We shall, together, reflect on what is being proposed, designed, and commercialized."

Max, half listening, studied Jorly closely.

"Today, we stand on the cusp of yet another era of unparalleled progress: one driven by the fusion of cutting-edge technology and the innate capacity of our brains. Recent studies have highlighted that what we understand and deem dangerous in the fields of cognitive enhancement may be far more subliminal and intrusive than we imagined. This week, it is both our opportunity and pleasure to come together to share our valuable expertise and insights on such matters."

In the stern atmosphere of the room, a woman sitting near Max broke the silence, whispering: "Jorly Benton... Yet one more person of extreme privilege trying to live responsibly in the world..."

Another guest responded, their voice carrying a reflective yet critical tone: "Perhaps the true challenge lies in accepting these blessings and transforming them into something else...?"

Jorly had almost no remaining connections with most of her family, who had all passed away. Why, then, should she feel responsible for their wrongdoings? Determined to shape her future and eager to engage critically with the world, she had returned to school in her late forties, enrolling in the Princeton Program of Religion, Ethics, and Politics. She had met Ghaner during a seminar entitled *Technology, Between Fantasy and Future Impacts*. From the beginning, their relationship was ambiguous and mysterious, yet, like any other business transaction, those who stood to gain the most ceased to question its nature.

"How can our knowledge, whether it be philosophy,

biotechnology, or even design, help shape the future of technology and ensure that cognitive enhancement, rather than reinforcing alienation, supports us in engaging with the world?" Ghaner pressed on, voice charged with intensity.

Jorly was standing silently beside him as if she were a product placement that had to stay in the camera's sight.

It seemed rehearsed, yet no one remained to be deceived: public funding was never an option for Ghaner's projects and endeavors, so it was left to dubious philanthropy to step in and invest in such programs.

For Jorly, there was only one condition: the conference needed to lead to tangible, practical outcomes. As a result, Ghaner agreed with her and the other organizers that the entire setup would result in a report, one that could be used for future decision-making and new legal perspectives, as well as eventually reassuring investors who demanded tangible feedback that was beyond intellectual stimulation.

To secure the delivery while cloaking it in legitimacy, they had invited an international ethics board to oversee and annotate the entire conference. Ghaner and Jorly knew that the practicality of such a report was limited and yet, the stakes were high.

"You have been invited to this event because you are, to the eye of the academic and intellectual world, a key component of these ongoing debates," Ghaner continued. "You are thinkers, makers, dreamers, and perhaps, already mind-enhanced!" he laughed.

"Together, we must strike a balance between innovation and ethical integrity, ensuring that technological endeavors do not only enhance some individual lives but also contribute positively to the well-being of the global community."

He stopped for a second and looked at the crowd with a prideful smile.

"For today, please connect, share your expertise and perspectives, and in the future days, take careful notes of the lectures and presentations. We look forward to meeting you all, separately, together, and why not first, at our after-dinner ceremony!"

They left the stage, followed by a series of applause.

Lost as if in a summer resort where little to no friendship yet existed, Max quickly left the hall and headed toward the elevators. There, she noticed for the first time the built-in LED panel, a silent sentinel announcing each speaker of the day. The black and white design displayed ambitious headshots of every lecturer, either present on-site or online, their names emblazoned in bold lettering, while the titles of their presentations appeared in elegant italics beneath. Each word, disappearing one after the other, resembled a disposable menu of humans' nichest topics and pursuits. At the top of the LED panel, Max saw a sticker of the heat-redistribution technology: *Dual Resolve*. The bold letters, rendered in Helvetica, showcased the logo of a striking red and pulsating hand, accented with blue highlights.

4.

When Max caught her reflection in the small bathroom mirror, she paused to rearrange her hair, pulling it back into a stricter, more composed style. She only had thirty minutes before the next activity: dinner time. Looking at herself reassuringly, she finally left the bedroom, trying to rehearse a few lines as she walked toward her destination. What to say, how to act, where to begin, yet the words remained stuck. Somehow, she was frozen by excitement and anxiety, unsure how to introduce herself or where even to start.

For as long as she could remember, Max had always nurtured a romantic notion of intellectuals and groundbreaking dinner conversations.

But that same evening, as she walked into the hall, she quickly realized that a gathering of people around a buffet was not a spectacle but a cacophony of chewing mouths and half-formed ideas, promptly consumed and digested and easily forgotten.

Max's gaze roamed the room, taking in every corner.

She settled into an empty chair beside a beautiful older woman, radiating confidence yet tinged with quiet displacement.

The woman stared at Max for a moment. Then, as if hoping to forge a silent pact, she extended her hand toward her direction.

"Elena."

"Max. Will you present some of your research?"

"Not really, no," she paused, "I'm Ghaner's wife."

At first, Max found it impossible to picture Ghaner walking alongside such a beautiful figure. She could never have imagined such a particular man in the company of an elegant and attractive person. But it wasn't just this image that unsettled her. Max vividly recalled a podcast she once listened to, where Ghaner had been interviewed about his career and life choices. Max particularly recalled the part where he discussed his teenage years and the realization that the unrequited love he harbored for his teenage best friend was more of a mental process than a physical one. A revelation that prompted him to contemplate the intricacies of the mind's capabilities in the absence of tangible reality. Ultimately, and in his own words: "it was this exploration that shaped his entire career," and so he restlessly delved deeper into this subject, sharing his insights through books and conferences of all kinds.

Sitting next to Elena, Max couldn't reconcile these two facts, wondering how men who seemed content with a simulated world rather than the real one still managed to find wives.

While pouring herself a glass of wine, and without even being asked, Elena explained how they had first crossed paths at a book launch in Aalborg, Denmark.

Elena, a young journalist at the time, had been invited by a friend. Seduced by the soft and docile melancholia in Ghaner's eyes, she dropped her phone number in between the lines as he signed the book she just bought.

"In the beginning, I tentatively explored the idea of dating this man, curious about what it might be like to sleep in the bed of such a brain," she claimed with a dry laugh. She recalled thinking by herself: "What do intellectuals talk about on dates? And later on, in their mundane lives?"

Elena had wondered if she, too, would become a muse or an object of study.

"But soon enough," she whispered, "I realized that the sparks of genius within Ghaner's brain only echoed within his mind and that often, loving this man felt like sitting down next to an autistic kid unable to take care of others' needs and spaces."

When Ghaner would get home, he would either pretend his research did not exist or dive into it so seriously that no one else around mattered.

As it seemed, Elena had learned to embrace the unspectacularness of marrying one of the world's most clever men, and the stillness that this choice implied.

"When we go out," Elena continued, "I can sometimes feel the weight of others' gazes, eyes, and ears discreetly lingering on me and my marriage. They probably wondered what it's like to be married to such a persona... Some might even question how a man like him ever found a wife."

Max sat still in silence.

Observing Elena's gentle and refined gestures, she couldn't help but wonder about the nature of the species unfolding before her mind's eye. Could a man who has perfected the art of self-gratification within the realms of his mind truly find the need for a partner? Maybe it was simply a strategic marketing maneuver. Perhaps Elena, too, derived benefits and satisfaction from such a partnership. After all, Ghaner was not in any way unattractive, and he undoubtedly enjoyed certain privileges.

Abruptly, Elena picked up her phone to show Max an old picture of Ghaner and her, all in black and white. There, she appeared, twenty years younger, a striking figure, exuding the gaze of a sharp, strategic woman. From the image alone, one could sense that Elena had once embodied femininity and the fragility of life and beauty in a manner that was ornamental, a performance that translated into scents and fantasies.

"Sorry. I should stop rambling about my life... Would you like something to drink, perhaps?" asked Elena.

"Water, please."

"Right," she paused. "Have you noticed how hot it has been? If I had not seen the snow this morning, I would have bet we're somewhere in Mallorca in July. I do not understand how this *Dual Resolve* thing functions... But perhaps, sometimes, technology works a little too well."

As Elena bent closer and poured water into the glass, Max re-examined her with growing curiosity. Her impeccably styled black hair was sleek and tightly secured. Sporting a fashion sense that blended elements of the corporate and artistic, she exuded an air of adaptability, as if she had mastered the art of navigating diverse spaces seamlessly. Her piercing green eyes left a lasting impression on those bold enough to meet her gaze for too long. Her radiance shone brighter than the brilliance of her man's mind.

In this carefully curated get-together, conversations and topics began to layer and intertwine, producing a curious mix of politics, ethics, potential sponsorships, and renewable energies.

Max observed the other guests in silence, unsure how and when her expertise would be of benefit. She noticed a fragile and petite figure that appeared to be of her age. The young woman appeared agile and lively, with a hint of mischief in her movements. There was something vaguely familiar about her, an unshakable sense of recognition, though Max couldn't quite place it.

As the young figure approached Elena, Max, who was still sitting next to her, pretended to reach for a fruit, subtly eavesdropping on their conversation.

"I'm so happy to see you here, Klara!"

"My pleasure," answered the young woman.

With her light brown eyes matching her hair and a subtle hint of lip gloss, Klara Suentes appeared strikingly unconventional, almost too fresh, too pretty, and too young or innocent for such an event.

Only the devil knew how hard she worked.

At twenty-seven, this brilliant and captivating genius had been invited to present an excerpt from her recently published PhD titled *A Substitute for Experiences: Lucidity Beyond Materiality.*

Klara's gaze held the sharpness of a predator and her tone of voice was as sharp as a knife. In her quest for ultimate clarity and research into the brain's infinite possibilities, Klara had given up on pills, supplements, drugs, antidepressants, coffee, alcohol, and anything that might cloud her mind. Her sobriety and clairvoyance emitted through every room.

Max observed her mutely, sensing an impressive yet problematic kind of dedication in her. The one that young women often adopt while struggling to carve out their own space as they are navigating perilous settings.

After greeting the other guests, Klara turned toward Max. An unspoken recognition passed between them.

They stared at each other for a moment before finally beginning to talk.

"Klara."

"Max. I heard you'll present a book?"

"You too, or so I've heard?"

"I guess you will soon find out," Max mumbled with mischief.

Klara answered with a flirtatious smile.

***

On her way back to her room, Max spotted the remains of what used to be a big window, now fully coated by the aluminum coverage of pipelines. Through the part that was not covered, she could detect the land of Svalbard, barely emitting light. On the outskirts, Max noticed the rays of artificial light fading into the darkness. Even in their faintest form, the dimmed bulbs allowed her eyes to trace the contours of a land blanketed in a soft layer of snow, ringed by endless mountains.

Overwhelmed by the sensation of a sudden claustrophobia and the complicated nature of a walk outside, she rushed to her room, wanting to wash away her anxieties.

While the cold water trickled down her waist and thighs, she tried to harness all the excitement, hope, and courage she had once felt about discovering Svalbard. The lofty feeling of being part of something bigger than herself. The dream of meeting like-minded individuals, exchanging ideas full of wonder and surprise.

Lying down in bed, she noticed how the heated air, which had been smooth and subtle the day before, had started to emit a peculiar, tickling whine.

She lay silently, half-naked on the single bed, gently removing the layers of bedding that had shielded her the previous night. She closed her eyes, hoping to soon fall asleep and wake up revived. Yet, the arrangement of the entire building haunted her.

Each human body, placed in its tiny sleeping box, isolated enough for rest, yet pressured and squeezed, with flows of heat and energies endlessly harvested through the pipelines.

5.

By the second morning, the growing heat and relentless ticking of the pipes had only intensified. Max wandered around the room, her eyes scanning for a controller of some kind, but her search turned up nothing.

The source of the ticking seemed to originate from the top corners of the room, but as Max moved closer, the sounds faded away, perpetually out of reach. Stifled by the stuffy air, she decided to visit the building's gym, hoping to find it empty.

She pushed the door and, to her great surprise, found herself alone in the basement. Working out never felt pleasant, but she knew satisfaction wasn't the point: it was about letting go of her fears. It wasn't that her body couldn't provide a sense of reward, but rather that the outcomes of somatic activities somehow left her disappointed, never quite living up to her expectations. It was the same on every occasion: underwhelmed while hiking in spring, unmoved during massages, and melancholic after sex. There were rare exceptions, moments that felt otherworldly, but they were so few and far between that relying on them felt like self-betrayal.

Max ran on the treadmill like a wild animal for an hour, then stepped away, momentarily freed from her anxieties.

***

Later that morning, when Max entered the conference space, Bill Niklay was already on stage, poised to unleash himself. Standing tall, exuding enthusiasm and pride, he resembled a genuine, trustworthy politician. The grey suit he wore reflected the stage's blue lights. Max imagined it would amplify the momentum of his speech. Behind his back, one could read, projected in bold letters:

PROGRESS IS NOT :

FEELING WITHOUT TOUCH

EXPERIENCING WITHOUT EVIDENCE

KNOWING WITHOUT LIVING

If Bill Niklay once believed in the possibilities of digital development, he had rapidly been disheartened by the absurd events held around California and the esoteric investments made in companies that, truly, no one, even himself, believed in. Once a tech enthusiast, he now commanded attention with his talks and writings on what he coined as *Technological Disenchantment*. The expression, although self-explanatory, always offered him the opportunity to tour conferences and symposiums, speaking about what he had seen, heard, and experienced throughout his career and life.

Over time, his mission had been evolving.

Currently, he was devoted to ensuring that technological progress was evaluated, regulated, and shaped in ways that were not only effective but also steered clear of the impossible and dystopian.

In his words, "the doomsday of a Matrix- or Inception-type simulation would never come: life, nature, technology, and economics were too fleeting and complex to harbor such wishes, especially considering the myriad of natural and geopolitical upheavals in the world!"

Bill knew that the real work was to deconstruct its tales and, instead, look at the mere facts.

"The scholarly discourse on mind, or cognitive enhancement, has now entered its third decade," stated Bill while opening his arms to the stage, "as posited at the inception of this research, the question of possibilities and causalities is complex. Enhancement and progress are, indeed, intrinsic to human nature, and both concepts have played a pivotal role in shaping our humanity. Yet, these are the exact lines on which technophilic strategists operate. Disenchantment with technological advancement..."

He paused.

"It is more of an exponential curve than a steady, linear path. Throughout my career, I have attended more than a hundred colloquiums and symposiums, endlessly fascinated by the cult-like scenarios surrounding these crowds, mostly equipped with men who, like I once did, daydreamed about the idea of alternative lives. Over time, I came to realize that these same CEOs often prioritized storytelling over efficient operations, consistently falling short whenever they stepped into the spotlight."

The crowd was perplexed.

"After all, haven't we all noticed the myriad of technical glitches, from microphone malfunctions to projector problems, casting serious doubts on the vision of a flawlessly executed technological future?"

A few participants laughed tensely.

"Coming back to the lineage of our topic... it is evident to acknowledge that efforts to enhance cognitive abilities often use traditional methods with long histories. For instance, the use of education and training to improve cognitive faculties like focus, memory, and analytical reasoning, while practices such as yoga, martial arts, meditation, and creativity workshops are commonly employed for mental training. So, surely, in that light, everything is cognitive enhancement."

The crowd was attentively listening, yet most of them seemed confused about the pessimistic nature of this opening talk.

"Pens, calculators, and then later on, personal computers were developed as technological tools to boost our cognitive abilities... and with this argument, it is easy to claim that cognitive and technological enhancement are inevitable, that it is an essential part of human progress. Because cognitive enhancement is a significant aspect of human nature, its expansion raises future concerns. A/R, V/R, brain-computer interface, Neural Lace, AI agents, and replicated lovers... Not everything is worth enhancing, and there should be an assessment of that said enhancement."

Bill harbored a deep-seated awareness that all the CEOs and investors he met took great care to keep their children from getting too close to the technological devices and tools they themselves had designed. He had accepted to join the conference because, for once, "it was about ethics!"

"I'm not scared of the metaverse taking over," he joked. "I am not scared of Google Glass becoming the new normal. Rather, I fear that technology, in its most delicate, transparent, and pervasive ways, is already changing the way people relate and understand the world.

While brain-computer interfaces and wearable devices may not yet be widely usable or commercialized, I argue that their development and eventual normalization raise many questionable paradigms, which I hope to explore with you throughout this timeline."

Max shortly looked around to observe the captivated audience, fidgeting and sweating in their seats.

She, too, couldn't help but keep moving about; her body was aching from her early-morning run. Max readjusted her trousers to check the state of her legs: a few veins seemed to have burst.

"Fuck," she whispered.

Could the mere act of running this morning have caused this?

"Of course, we want to upgrade!" Bill exclaimed, pacing the stage, his voice sharp with agitation as slides and images flashed behind him. "But we shall question the necessity of developing such technologies beyond bare improvement, and, more precisely, have a specific look at who it will benefit."

Max caressed her bruised leg. She was ever only engaging in physical activities for the sake of a possible catharsis. By far, her favorite machine was the treadmill. There was a faintly romantic, almost fictional appeal to a device that spared one from the world, yet simulated motion within that same world. It was an easy commitment to make, an easy action to push herself into, and even easier to withdraw from.

Secretly, Max wanted a love like that machine: controlled and constant. A love-space in which she could enter smoothly, choose the pace, and select the obstacles. A straightforward path toward something she could control, something she could always opt out of. An object that did not shed light on her fallout.

"Together, how can we ensure, through regulations and ethics, that the pursuit of enhancement advances in a positive and caring manner, rather than leading us to despise the natural state of our bodies and our nature?" Bill concluded, taking a moment to let his words sink in.

The crowd erupted into applause.

The sound of the animated hands brought Max back to where she was.

The screen on stage displayed in big and bold letters the screenshot of a Wired article from over ten years ago: "I Am Once Again Asking Our Tech Overlords to Watch the Whole Movie."

The energy in the room shifted as people began to laugh softly, their appreciation growing louder with each passing second.

Max looked backward and noticed Elena glaring at her from afar. Her expression warned of trouble, quiet but insistent, cautious.

***

That night, Max chose a spot at the corner of the long, rectangular dinner table, hoping to keep conversations to a minimum. Despite the growing heat, she found that the atmosphere was surprisingly jovial, with acquaintances and familiar faces already beginning to form.

Jona and Amos spotted Max from a distance and settled nearby.

She offered a half-smile.

"You look great," Amos suggested.

"Thanks," Max answered with a dry tone.

Amos's gaze locked onto Max's as if he were waiting for her to give in.

When she finally looked back, his gaze dropped a few centimeters down.

"I did not notice that necklace before."

"Well, we only met yesterday."

"What does it represent?"

"It's just a cycle, split into two parts by a simple line," whispered Max while touching the tiny silver object.

"There should be an esoteric researcher to enlighten us here..." Jona said, a cynical smile tugging at his lips as he edged toward the object.

"I don't think it means anything," snapped Max before tucking it inside her shirt. "I found it on the ground as I was strolling in the streets of Vienna."

As she extended her arms to replace the jewellery, a few bruises became visible, exposing the skin underneath.

"Did you wrestle with someone already?" said Jona, smirking.

Max stared at the stains of color on her skin, unsure of how they had appeared. She was incapable of explaining its whys.

"Max?" insisted Jona.

An elegant woman, who had been quietly listening while sitting to their right, suddenly interrupted.

"Perhaps you should stop insisting on answers?"

Max turned around and spotted the familiar face she

had been hoping to see: Astrid Burman.

Renowned for being both exceptionally talented and difficult to handle, Astrid carried a courage and consistency few could match. Critics often dismissed her methodologies as too experimental, her arguments as insufficiently scientific, yet her credentials in psychology and economics spoke for themselves: she had the knowledge and experience to excel in any field. In recent years, Astrid had gained popularity for exploring the power of imagination and speculation, and how these faculties, when amplified by digital tools, could increase disconnection from reality, creating what she calls the *phantasm industry.*

While Max always devoured her theories and arguments, her latest book, *Digital Lives and Desire: Capitalizing on the Symbolic Economy,* stirred more controversy than interest. Critics found it lacking in theoretical rigor and claimed that it was overly speculative, hard to read, and too experimental.

Astrid bent toward Max to shake her hand, to which she whispered with the wide-eyed gaze of a fan: “I’m Max.”

6.

At night, the high-pitched hum of the pipes buzzed through the air, filling the room and keeping Max wide awake. This time, the unsettling sound carried with it a new, ominous smell of burning plastic.

Max stared at the picture framed on the wall.

Printed there, an image of Svalbard in the summer, proud as a striking reminder of Arctic beauty. The golden glow of the midnight sun bathed the scene in a warm, ethereal light, softening the icy blues of the fjord below. In the foreground, the delicate greens of the tundra and tiny wildflowers seemed to breathe life into the landscape as Max had come to know it. The photograph oozed both serenity and wildness as if it were a portal to a distant, untouched world. On the wall, the image stood out vividly, casting a sense of calm and endless space over the room.

Max pondered why a space that was deprived of windows and light would need such a testimony of life. Perhaps, she thought, in the long periods of dark and cold, the only thing to look forward to was the belief of a spring that had yet to arise.

In an evasive dream, Max was sitting across from Astrid at the dinner table. The security guard from the airport and Elena were chatting on the side. Together, they stared at Max, murmuring secrets she could not intercept.

"What is this about?" Max demanded, confused.

They looked at each other before turning away, whispering a few words that only Max could hear: "The symbol on her necklace. It suggests bringing the formal and informal worlds together, all through this middle line."

Confused, Max adjusted the necklace again, her fingers instinctively reaching to fix the hidden piece of jewelry beneath her T-shirt. The cold silver pressed lightly against her skin, reminding her that it was a symbol she had never truly selected, but perhaps, in some subtle, inexplicable way, it had claimed her.

When she took her hand away, Elena lunged at her, yanking the necklace from her neck.

Max woke up in a jolt, still stuck in the same room.

Sweating, desperate for air, and with no window to open, she got up and tried to convince her sleep-deprived body that it was the perfect opportunity to get back on the treadmill. But when she arrived, she realised that by this third morning, word of the hidden workout space had already spread, and to Max's discomfort, she wasn't the only one there.

Changing in the gym, Max found herself thinking that harvesting human heat wasn't as absurd as it first seemed. After all, maybe it was a brilliant idea to use all this intellectual and bodily matter for a concrete purpose. In that way, they wouldn't merely consume and take but generate and produce as well.

Moving toward her favorite treadmill, Max noticed the absurd and humorous portraits of all these clever, esteemed individuals again. Finally undressed, moving like enchained rats. The restless, sweating bodies before her triggered a rush of connections between all the elements.

The flesh, the brain, the sweat, and the pipelines, now forever connected through the fabric of the building and the tissues of life.

She started the machine and closed her eyes. There was no determination left in her, no specific energy or desire, so to fuel her motivation, she thought of all the times she had hoped for something to heal her, change her, pushing herself harder with each step.

Shortly after she started running, a growing pain and tension lodged in her pelvis and transferred to her legs, prompting her to stop. Yet she moved forward, driven to prove the strength of her will, running until she soared off the end of the treadmill.

***

In the conference room, Ilo, who was also late, took a seat close to Max. She leaned in and whispered gently: "How is everything?"

Max nodded.

"It's okay," she paused. "My sleeping isn't the best, though. Perhaps it's due to the absence of daylight."

"Would you rather have had this event in full bright light? That's just another kind of insanity, trust me."

Max scrutinized Ilo.

"Svalbard only offers extremes, it seems," added Ilo.

"But we're right at the end of the polar night season. From now on, it can only get better."

The temperature had slowly started rising again.

"Why is it so warm?"

"You weren't there during the tour?"

"I was. Just not fully listening,"

"We're harvesting human heat and redistributing it through the building," explained Ilo. "The main timber structure was largely prefabricated to avoid thermal bridges and heat loss, which is why it might be a little hard to breathe or too warm at times."

"Yeah, that I remember," Max replied. "But how?"

Max attentively waited for Ilo's words as Jona walked up to the stage and snatched the microphone.

"As technology increasingly merges with our physical and personal lives, designers need to recognize the impact of these advancements."

Projected in the background, images of his portfolio and past collaborations were moving left and right.

"For years, I have explored how the interface, traditionally seen as a bridge between human bodies and external entities, has shifted in significance with the advancement of contemporary technology. My career as a designer in some of the most advanced and established tech companies has led me, over time, to reconsider the boundaries between usability and addiction, practicality and intrusion."

Max looked at him for a moment, radiating on stage, but her mind wandered to the possibility of a longer conversation with Ilo.

"What happened to the windows?" continued Max quietly, looking at the ceiling and corners of the room.

"Ah," whispered Ilo, "most of them have been replaced with panels that allow for the pipes to go in and out. We concealed them, once again, to minimize heat loss. As I said, for the experiment to work, we had to produce this sort of airtight building envelope. That's why you will find airlock doors between any outside entry or exit, and barely any functioning windows."

Two unknown figures turned around, casting threatening gazes at Max and Ilo, demanding silence.

In the background, Jona was still proceeding with keywording and slides.

"When crafting new technologies, whether the interface is embodied or aims to influence our cognitive processes, we must extend our considerations beyond mere functionality. It is imperative to move beyond the pursuit of polished experiences and embrace a deeper understanding of technology's impact on our minds and its overall transparency."

"Is that also why the bedroom ceilings are so low?"

"Yes," answered Ilo with an audacious smile, trying to lower her voice to a barely audible frequency. "Achieving uniform heat distribution across the entire building has proven to be quite complex. So for this experiment, we concentrated the heat harvesting in the dining and conference rooms and redistributed the captured energy to the smaller remaining spaces. In the best-case scenario, and if the heat-forecasting system functions correctly, the temperature between the spaces should self-regulate."

"Are there rooms where the heat isn't distributed to?" murmured Max.

"Yes. Mine, for example," answered Ilo softly. "But they're not accessible to the general public, or we closed them just to make sure the hot air does not get lost."

Ilo looked at Max playfully. She gently signaled for her to hush, whispering: "I can tell you more later."

When Max's eyes finally found the stage, Jona was

still showing various slides of wearable technologies and implants. His argument was loud and clear: embedding the interface into physical bodies would make the technological object effectively disappear, seamlessly integrating into the fabric of physical existence.

"Imagine," Jona declared, "Everything that you hate. Notifications, likes, hateful comments, and bad reviews. All of this, but so much closer to your body, to your brain, perhaps even located within your skin."

For a brief instant, Max tried to envision such a plausible future, but her peripheral vision kept drifting to Ilo's hands.

"It is time to integrate viable principles into the development process of cognitive technologies, making sure that such tools don't become intrusive and, at worst, invasive," reinforced Jona.

Dehydrated from the rising heat, Max grabbed a bottle of water from her right side. Trying to take several sips at once, she choked slightly and coughed a little too loudly, drawing attention to herself.

"This should end soon," claimed Ilo.

Max tried to swallow the thick air, but her coughing grew stronger. She sounded like a wounded animal.

Then, a few droplets of moisture slowly fell from the ceiling, landing on her arms. In a swift motion, she sprang from her chair and hurriedly made her way toward the exit.

With her hands covering her mouth, she collected Jona's final words as she walked out, Ilo on her side.

"While delving into this consideration may unravel complexities, I conclude today's short lecture by stressing that the body and the brain aren't mere conduits for delivering experiences but, rather, the site where experiences must unfold."

As Ilo pressed against the exit door, parts of the crowd turned around, staring at the young figures departing.

***

Max silently followed Ilo from the conference room to the airlocked entrance. There, Ilo grabbed two huge jackets from the pile that was left aside. Constantly accompanied by the whistling songs of the ventilation pipes, Ilo said: "It might take a minute for your body to acclimate to the temperature change."

Max got dressed as Ilo was pushing aside all the locks and air-caps, entering a password that Max caught a glimpse of from the corner of her eye. As Ilo was opening the locker, Max glanced at the multiple guns, all neatly aligned.

"Gloves, perhaps?" Ilo wondered with a smile.

When Ilo touched Max's finger, she glanced at her in surprise.

"Wow," breathed Ilo. "Why are your fingers so cold?"

"It's always been like this," answered Max, flashing a shy smile.

Ilo grabbed Max's hands tightly, attempting to warm them up.

"Are you even alive?" said Ilo with a mischievous smile.

When Ilo finished putting on her outfit and loading the weapon, she reassured Max: "It's not as scary as one might think."

She gently pushed the door open to the endless darkness of Svalbard.

As they walked, the crunching snow beneath their shoes and the dim glow from the streetlights were their only guides. A few minutes of silence and some uneasy walking later, Ilo pointed to what resembled a bench, suggesting that Max sit down.

"If I need more of this, do I have to ring you every time?"

"I guess so." Ilo smiled."That being said, my doors are always open for incoming deliveries and guests, but only once in the morning, and once at night."

Sitting in the sea of dimness, with only a few lights remaining as proof of life, Ilo started to recount how the experimental construction had originated.

Jorly Benton and the architect Paul Nachman previously knew each other, but only from a distance. They had randomly crossed paths at a conference on Smart Systems and Climate Change in Oslo. Rumors circulated that, after a few drinks, both had become slightly inebriated beside the corner of the conditioned air booth. Amid their tipsy musings, they began speculating about a central heating system powered by human warmth, redistributed throughout a designated area. In the context of impending global warming, they trusted that experimenting with forecasting systems and heat redistribution could easily be funded, yet not so easily designed. For Paul Nachman, who wanted to experiment with human heat, there was no better testing ground than the icy and cold-hearted winds of Svalbard.

"And what a place to do it," Ilo added.

Previous research and experiments had been conducted at the Oslo Architecture University, where Ilo happened to be an exchange student at the time. She had the opportunity to work on a small-scale experiment of such a building, and Paul, who had been teaching there as a professor at the time, invited her to work on a similar project in Svalblard a few years later.

"A delirium," gasped Max.

"Watch your mouth," said Ilo, laughing. "It could be brilliant if it happens to work out."

7.

"So it does not work?" asked Max, troubled.

"It's complicated," sighed Ilo, "the air indoors must meet the outside air, and only then can it be altered through recuperation mechanisms. But for that, we need even more heat protection. That is also why we focused strongly on insulation and using non-conductive materials like wood surfaces and fabrics of all kinds. I'll draw something for you." Ilo took a pen and a piece of paper out of her pocket. "Usually, heat is captured through the air with the pipelines from what we call 'high-level human heat'. This is done where most people gather. In our case, it is the lecture room or the dining room. The warm air is then sent to an energy recovery device, which contrasts it with the outside air. It is then stored through energy storage and sent back to be redistributed among different rooms and spaces through a forecasting controller."

"Forecasting?"

"It is quite difficult to tell how warmth is redistributed

in spaces and whether it will move, evaporate rapidly, or stick around. Advanced systems use forecasting to optimize where heat will be needed. But the controller we designed here is particularly complex and tedious to use. Experimental."

"And only you can work with that?"

"Well, if things go wrong, there's little I can do. At best, I can try to outsmart the controller and address any detected heat loss. But so far, my main responsibility is sending updates to Paul about the overall air quality and humidity, and managing any drastic heat changes if they ever appear. As long as it's manageable, we keep the experiment running."

"Are we guinea pigs for an architect's and a philanthropist's deliriums?"

"I would not phrase it like that," Ilo paused. " But, yes. It's experimental."

She paused again.

"When Ghaner initially pitched Jorly about his conference topic, she was struck by the idea of combining these two experimental events. In her own words, there was 'something both epic and absurd about the connection of two inherently disconnected, almost-too-far-stretched topics'. The one of the mind, and the one of the body, one about its presence and the other about its absence. She was going to fund both, so she proposed that Ghaner use the building for free if he agreed to try out the architectural concept. When Ghaner read her proposal, he did not hesitate. For Paul, it was a win-win too. A first big-scale model, which, if successful, could be prototyped for more prospects in the next few years."

"And if it does not work?"

"Nothing much," laughed Ilo. "At worst, it'll be a little too warm and hard to breathe. You'll survive."

Max stood still, bewildered yet captivated.

"Experiments like *Dual Resolve* may seem like a stretch, but the concept of heat redistribution already exists in many buildings. The Hortus Botanicus in Amsterdam uses a similar energy exchange system with the nearby Hermitage Museum. Excess heat from the Hermitage is transferred via long pipes to the greenhouse, where it's used to maintain ideal growing conditions through a heat pump. The cooled water is then sent back to the Hermitage for air conditioning."

"Sure," Max laughed ironically. "But in our case, it's freezing, and we're in the middle of the Arctic."

Ilo replied with a calming and soothing smile before handing the finished sketch of the building to Max.

Ilo appeared as a guardian of a castle or a secret dynasty, a place only she could control. In the silent nightscape, Max and Ilo faced the desperately dark horizon, with only a few lights, the Science Center standing as a testament to life. In this gloomy cinematic stillness, the wind howling through the hills left Max feeling at a loss. As if she had no repertoire to draw from, no sense of what to feel in the overwhelming presence of such untouched nature.

She looked at Ilo.

Ilo, on the contrary, seemed to thrive, as in a state of mindfulness. With her eyes closed and her body fully present, she seemed to find tranquility amid the surrounding nothingness, wearing a smile that defied any signs of anxiety or worry. Seated on the bench, she resembled a glowing idol, recharged by the strength of the cold and the harsh winds.

When Ilo finally opened her eyes, she met Max's gaze, which was confused and insecure.

"The view feels nice, right?"

"I guess," answered Max.

Max tried to recall the last time she had encountered a view that left her breathless. There was an almost sad flatness of reaching the summit of a hill or the culmination of a hike, as if the exertion itself or the anticipation sustained her, leaving the final vista feeling like a hollow promise, devoid of the intended enchantment.

Sometimes, while running on the treadmill, Max would close her eyes and envision forests, scents, and sounds she had not yet encountered in this life. More than nature itself, the faithful recreation of a natural space in her mind always kept her walking and running a little longer.

"Never moved by landscapes?" asked Ilo.

Another memory washed over her like a bitter wave, taking her back to the dry lands and towering pines of the Alps. Holidays organized by her grandmother replayed in her mind, with her older brother by her side, both of them determinedly trekking with their backpacks. She recalled the endless hikes toward destinations that sparked their curiosity, though she struggled to remember what truly guided her along the way. Perhaps it was only her grandmother's unwavering encouragement that had propelled her forward.

"Not that I recall, no," answered Max, as if shamefully admitting that she'd always been a virgin.

Drawn back into her memories, Max found other traces and images of these summer hikes. Often, at the precise moment of arrival, when it was time to pause, observe, and surrender to exhaustion, Max found herself feeling empty and bewildered as if gazing upon the hollow projection of a ghostly screen. Nature overwhelmed her. She hadn't learned to appreciate it or yearn for it. Every shape from afar felt so distant, so flat, painted away. When she would finally arrive, whether at a serene lake or atop a majestic mountain, she would gaze out at the view, feeling a mix of disappointment and detachment.

Max turned away from Ilo.

“Do you think you could get touched by a projected image or memory in your mind?”

“What do you mean?” asked Ilo.

“As if I could send you a view, or a moment, and you could see it all through my eyes.”

Ilo seemed perplexed, unswayed. “I’m not sure. We would have to try.”

Max felt the urge to reply. “You probably would,” as if it were impossible to say otherwise, but no words came out of her mouth. She was frozen, body, mind, and heart. Was there any point in pretending that the simple joys of sight were enough, or
in feigning the feelings and happiness brought about by mere observation?

Max wondered if she ought to have said something more banal.

When Ilo noticed Max’s sudden lack of attention, she decided to shorten their outside stay.

“It’s about time to head back,” she offered, smiling. “We should make it to dinner on time.”

***

From the far end of the dinner table, Max could hear the echo of a heated conversation. In between bites and sips, and while referencing various research projects from the MIT Media Lab and an unknown policy agency, the group of individuals struggled to find any friendly agreement.

A peculiar feeling washed over Max as she observed

these bodies, so real and so hungry, some of them sweaty and pungent, debating esoteric and distant futures. Unbothered to dissect the conversation, Max looked away, biting into the Brunost cheesecake while observing Klara, who was savoring her fourth glass of Cloudberry. Max watched her gestures and manners for an instant.

"Having fun?" Klara looked at her.

"Sort of," said Max. "Are you?"

"I am."

Klara's presence held an elusive quality, as if she wanted to be seen, yet from a certain distance. She was not attending lectures and could only be seen around the building in the evenings, like a late-night bird that hides during the daytime.

Max wasn't immune to her mysterious charms for reasons she couldn't quite explain. She felt a sense of camaraderie toward her. After all, they were the only two young women in this theater of lights. Still, Max couldn't quite understand why Klara's research was particularly relevant to the framework of the conference. Lucid dreaming was, indeed, the ultimate natural brain hack, but it was a mode that did not require external technology.

"I've always wondered," Max paused, "are lucid dreamers doing okay?"

"What do you mean?" Klara said bluntly.

"It must be tiring to live two separate lives fully, every day and every night."

Klara laughed. Her cat-shaped eyes flashed, as if perceiving Max in a new light.

"You're right," answered Klara before finishing her drink. "They're not fine."

***

On the way back to her room, Max briefly passed by the lounge space, catching sight of one of the reporters in conversation with Jona. There was something about the reporter's posture, a slight hunch, a nervous glance, that suggested he was trying to blend into the background. Jona nodded in silence several times.

"If you ask me... I don't think we need guidelines. We need laws. We need sanctions. Companies do not change unless you force them to."

When their gaze met, Max's eyes apparently suggested an invitation for further discussion. Jona waved at her, but she feigned to misinterpret it and continued walking down the hallway.

In the corridor, far from the distant brouhahas, the high-pitched whispering of the pipes echoed louder.

As she approached her room, Max pondered the possibility of reaching rest and sleep throughout the night: she felt suffocated before even opening the door. With the urge to seek refuge in another space, Max turned around and started to walk in the opposite direction, where she knew the cooks, the technicians, and Ilo lived. Max hurried toward this unknown destination, guided by the humming sound of the heat controller, its melody growing louder with every step.

When she finally came across the door marked with Ilo's name, Max froze.

Overcome by fear but driven by an even stronger desire, she decided to knock.

8.

Ilo opened the door, cheeks rising just a touch in surprise.

Max walked in, a sudden spark of life rekindling within her spine. The room, painted with tones of beige and wooden fabrics, filled with succulents and small souvenirs, evoked a sense of care and rest that Max couldn't quite place.

"I'm sorry, it's a little messy right now," whispered Ilo with a grin.

Max smiled and patiently observed Ilo rearranging the many items and objects decorating her habitat. They all seemed to come from different places, perhaps different lives, yet they coexisted perfectly in this realm, Ilo's realm.

The room resembled that of a child, with a ladder leading up to a cozy loft with a bed on the right side.

Here, amid Ilo's treasures, Max thought for a second that she had found a refuge, a place to hide that offered an unexpected and immediate warmth, a sense of belonging, a comforting embrace that made it easier to breathe and relax.

"The temperature feels different here."

"Indeed," responded Ilo. "The room is rather close to the heat storage, so to avoid a thermal bust, we decided to leave it without the redistribution device."

Max's gaze was traveling around, overwhelmed by the amount of stuff and traces of life. On the wall hung an arrangement of different collages and images, drawings, and sketches from the past. Her eyes stopped on a black-and-white picture of three individuals playing around with ventilation pipelines. Max could discern the figure of an old man, accompanied by another agile figure at his side.

"When was that?"

"That? That's back when I worked with Paul on the building."

"What's he like?" asked Max, still staring at the image.

"Well. He's a genius, that's for sure. The kind of architect who has read too much science fiction, and has the network and technical knowledge to make it work somehow."

Ilo turned around, noticing the scrutiny in Max's eyes, who was still staring at the picture.

"What?" Ilo asked, gently smiling.

"How come you seem to be so good at this?"

"At what?"

"Fixing. Building. Being."

Ilo paused for a moment.

"I'm not sure. It might sound weird, but sometimes, it feels like I have had multiple chances and opportunities to live life already. I guess that, after a while, you get better at it."

"So you've died before?"

"I think so. Many times."

Ilo was chopping some ginger and lemon when Max

suddenly asked: "What does it feel like, dying?"

"Ah..." sighed Ilo.

Max looked at the picture, patiently waiting for an answer.

"Do you know that poem by Angie Sijun Lou? It's called 'Jessica Gives Me a Chill Pill'."

Max didn't say a word.

"It goes: 'Jessica has a forehead scar from the deep end of a pool. I ask Jessica what drowning feels like, and she says not everything feels like something else.'"

"What do you mean by that?"

"I guess not every experience can be shared, imported, compared, or even described. You have to see for yourself."

When Ilo turned back to Max, she was still staring at the picture, as if moved by what had been said.

"Are you staying?"

"No, sorry, I think I need to get back," Max said, making her way toward the door.

"You know you can always come back," Ilo offered, eyes full of care. "Just knock three times."

***

Walking back to her room, Max could feel her initial excitement fading away. The visions and possibilities of future encounters, fabulations, and opportunities were slowly dissipating. Once so enthusiastic about the idea of being part of such an intellectual and ethical enterprise, she now regretted being physically present on site. The intellectual thrive and historical momentum she had pictured grandly turned out to be little more than a fantasy, a fleeting mirage.

Instead, the all-too-human traits of the guests and

speakers laid bare their banalities and inconsistencies.

Their only common denominator was that they were all, including Max, stuck in the same place, frozen in time.

Strolling through the sealed corridor, Max longed for a space where she could hide and never return from. Slowly, her boiling thoughts, accompanied by the humming and whistling of the pipes, crumpled up like the ball of hyper-awareness she hadn't felt in a while.

This was the kind of alertness to potential danger that kept her awake, unable to fall asleep at night. From the tenseness of her breast, Max knew she was reaching the end of her menstrual cycle, her mind caught in a limbo of hormonal and psychological turmoil. On those nights, death held no significance.

Instead, it felt as though she was merely waiting for an excuse to commit a crime.

Anxious and restless, Max lay down on her bed, searching for the small blade with her hand.

The hidden weapon felt too far to reach, inaccessible, displaced.

She pushed her arm deeper under the bed frame, trying to find the small object. Max wished to sleep with the knife held close to her heart, clutching it as tenderly as she would a beloved teddy bear. Lying in her quilted armor, a phrase from Jeanette Winterson came to her mind: "When she bleeds, the smells I know change color. There is iron in her soul... She smells like a gun."

She imagined that on those nights, she probably smelled like a knife.

***

On the fourth morning, Max, once again awake for far too

long, arrived a little earlier than usual. In the conference space, she found Klara and Ghaner meticulously preparing her presentation, checking each slide with careful precision. From this angle, they seemed innocent, two simple humans fumbling with how to best Airdrop the Keynote file from one machine to another, or simply set up the correct USB format. On the screen, the sentence 'A Substitute for Experiences' appeared, reminiscent of a billboard advertisement.

When the room had finally filled up and everyone was seated, Klara introduced herself, speaking sharply yet softly. She acknowledged that her presentation could appear somewhat off-topic, speculative, or perhaps not sufficiently critical. She stated her intentions of discussing the possibilities of healing with and through technologies, and how lucid dreaming could, facilitated with machinery, aid in this.

The crowd appeared doubtful but curious, attentive to each of her words.

As expected, Klara's recital felt seductively dominant. With a grin, she looked at the audience, pondering out loud: "So, what role do dreams play in cognitive enhancement?"

Klara had begun training for lucid dreaming during the early days of the COVID-19 lockdown. When she figured that the pandemic was going to last for a little while, she had decided to generate some fun for herself.

It did not take long to start working.

"Truth be told, I always possessed a vivid imagination and would occasionally experience lucid dreams," Klara claimed, "but some people are really... meant for this. Predisposed."

Klara had sensed that this alternative form of world-building was something she had to investigate: "The depth of sadness and heartbreak I had felt in my dreams surpassed anything I experienced in waking life."

The fear she encountered while sleeping was unparalleled, and the pleasures as well. Considering this mere observation and training, coupled with a bit more practice and technologies, the possibilities were endless, she argued: "Lucid dreaming holds promises across multiple domains, from aiding in the therapy of phobias and PTSD to fostering creativity, and potentially even improving athletic performance."

Max was no stranger to the practice of lucid dreaming. Opening doors to creativity and insights, remembering dreams and defusing nightmares, and reconnecting with lost loved ones. The promises were huge, but having tried it, Max worried about losing the ability to distinguish between night and day.

"Could lucid dreaming become a democratic and accessible form of technological therapy?" Klara continued, energetically presenting articles and scientific papers showing that researchers had experimented with using transcranial electrical brain stimulation to induce such states.

"As one can see, there exists a success rate of 58% with 25 Hz stimulation and 77% with 40 Hz stimulation."

Virtual reality, too, she showed, had also been utilized to simulate the potential of achieving a lucid dream-like state.

Looking at the crowd, her gaze piercing theirs, the dynamic young woman pondered: "How could lucid dreaming, considered an inherent technology of the brain and augmented by other devices, help individuals navigate complex, challenging, or even traumatizing experiences?"

Displaying screenshots of successful research projects, Klara introduced the crowd to what she assessed as two potential but still realistic scenarios. In a dystopian twist, companies could release affordable device gear that allowed people to induce lucid dreams easily. Driven by mundane human desires, many would use it for instant gratification, escaping into dreams of power, wealth, lust, and pleasure, leading to a growing detachment from reality as real-world crises worsened.

In her preferred, more optimistic scenario, society would anticipate these drawbacks and guide the technology toward constructive uses: "These advancements, if well orchestrated, could revolutionize how we approach mental health treatments and personal development, offering unprecedented insight into the inner workings of the mind and its potential for growth and healing. I wish to live in the best possible world where, if developed with ethics, technologies will enable us to experience better and greater lives."

When Klara abruptly concluded her talk, the crowd burst into applause so enthusiastically that it left little room for any potential critical feedback.

Max sat there, immobile. In a desperate attempt to find Ilo, she skimmed the room with her eyes, but Ilo was nowhere to be found.

***

On her way out toward the lounge, Max saw Klara and Ghaner, who appeared to be engrossed in a lively post-presentation debate. When Ghaner spotted Max, he gestured in her direction, inviting her to join.

She approached them politely, standing silently next to them as she attempted to listen intently to their animated conversation.

Ghaner was speaking vividly and rapidly, referencing with enthusiasm recent articles about the neural representation of observed, imagined, and attempted actions in the cortex of peculiar individuals.

Klara chimed in, supporting his points by mentioning how brain-computer interfaces could aid in differentiating and better understanding the difference between these processes.

“Fascinating, isn’t it, Max?” Ghaner pondered, “I imagine that this relates to your research as well.”

Klara glanced at Max, hoping for an instant response.

“I’m not sure,” Max answered shortly. “I wish I were better at acting upon, rather than imagining life.”

Her response left Klara and Ghaner stunned for a while.

Then, Klara shortly replied: “Well, people should focus on what they do best, right?”

“Max, I haven’t had a chance to speak with you yet,” interjected Ghaner. “How about meeting in my office before your presentation?”

Under different circumstances, Max would have declined such a last-minute, impromptu meeting. However, in that instant, she found herself unable to come up with a justifiable excuse.

What else could she possibly be occupied with? She had nowhere else to go.

Wrapped in a wave of politeness and performance, she nodded and replied: “Nine?”

“Well, tomorrow is the first conversational meeting,” answered Ghaner. “What about the day after?”

Max smiled and nodded politely before heading out.

***

At night, when Max entered the dining room, she was delighted to find an empty seat right next to Ilo.

Noticing Max's unusual smile, Amos decided to join the two women, sitting beside them. A moment of silence followed as he peered into Ilo's eyes, seemingly waiting for Max to introduce him.

"Ilo, this is Damos. Damos, this is Ilo."

"Wow," laughed Amos. "Still spelling my name wrong... You're one of a kind."

Ilo did not say a word but forced a smile, not specifically eager to have him stay.

In a moment of playful awkwardness, Amos attempted to pursue: "So... you're the tech support, right?"

"This and other things, yes," answered Ilo bluntly.

"Well. I don't mean to be rude..." stated Amos, "And I know you're not responsible for this... but it's getting kinda hot in here. And don't get me wrong... I like a little sweat. But this temperature is just not ideal for focusing."

Ilo stared back at him, silently.

"Thanks for the feedback," she claimed. "This operation is still in its preliminary stages and has not yet been optimized. While we have conducted some previous simulations, real-world conditions, like this one, are necessary to develop the technology. For now, it is important to maintain the current redistribution process to better understand its distribution system. Only then can we refine and refine it."

Amos cast a wary glance at Ilo before responding: "Thank God we're not spending a month in this fucking building."

He quickly excused himself, moving to another conversation at the far end of the table.

Heated from all sides, the room seemed to pulse with a life of its own, yet somehow Max's meal had already grown cold, covered in beads of moisture as if it had been left in a slow cooker, damp and unappetizing.

As she tried to eat one last bite, Ilo bent toward her, whispering in her ear: “Do you know how I realized that I was not into men?”

Max beamed while shaking her head.

“I never, ever, remember their name.”

9.

On the morning of the fifth day, Max was lying on a couch in the corridor near the meeting-room door, immobile, her computer resting in her left hand. The cold coffee in her right one as a half-hearted attempt to shake off the remnants of another sleepless night. Exhaustion was written all over her: the dark circles under her eyes, the halting rhythm of her speech, and the subtle trembling in her legs and arms. An unknown, mischievous guest who was also waiting for the doors to open was standing on her right side.

"Do you want one?" the unfamiliar face asked Max, offering her a pill.

"What is that?" she replied, eyeing it with suspicion.

"Piracetam. It's just a stimulant."

Max stared at the woman and her pill, bluntly.

"Come on," claimed the stranger, "isn't it exhausting, listening to people talk all day like that?"

"Is it a drug?" asked Max.

"No, I just told you. It'll make your mind a little sharper."

"I don't need this," Max said, looking once more at the pill.

"Oh, please," asserted the woman. "As far as I know, this isn't about the regulations of bio-hacking."

When Ghaner opened the door to the meeting room, the accumulated crowd was met with a strange smell of humidity and stale air. The space was full of heat and moisture as if it had occupied and not previously freshened up.. Nobody said anything, but from the expressions on their faces, Max could tell they had reached an unspoken consensus: heat redistribution was not the right technology for this site.

As everyone sat down at the circular table, Max needed a moment to observe all of them before realizing she, too, was now under scrutiny. She adjusted her seat and her hair, hoping to blend into the background for a while. She grabbed the leaflet of *Dual Resolve,* lying on the table in front of her, to put it aside. Across the room, Ilo stood watch like a lone guard, smiling at Max from a distance.

"Thank you for attending the first report meeting of the week," Ghaner began. "This session is meant for us to share concerns and thoughts on the event so far, and for the reporters to begin drafting their insights. We do not expect you to resolve any of the ongoing debates or issues just yet. This is simply a space to allow our critical minds to explore beyond the confines of presentations and lectures."

Max scrutinized the reporters seated closely beside her. They could almost be taken for outsiders in a setting that wasn't theirs, as if they had been invited to a performance without knowing their roles. Concealed behind their pencils, notes, and computers, Max realized she had never truly learned their names, nor heard their voices, save perhaps once. Their faces, most often expressionless, would only sometimes change to display perplexity or confusion about terminology. They seemed mentored, manufactured.

Unreal.

Jorly, too, was sitting in the corner of the room, still as a safeguard. She appeared a little more tense, a little less flexible than usual.

In the warm and quiet room, Ghaner cut through the silence again: "For now, has there been any conflict of interests or key component that we can already formulate, or start reflecting upon?"

A voice crackled through the computer, cutting through the murmurs that were responding to Ghaner.

"Ghaner, thanks for organizing this and curating this. I could not come here physically, but I've been following the recordings online. Perhaps I'm confused because I'm not on site... But I'd like to know what exactly we're focusing on here. It is still a little... unclear."

While the sharp, digital voice continued its speech, Max scanned every possible corner of the rounded table, which seemed to form a perfect cycle. For the first time, she could see them all, face to face, with nowhere to hide. The online commentator's remarks left a few speakers with annoyed and irritated expressions, but they politely waited for him to finish his thoughts.

"Lucid dreaming, mind enhancement in everyday life, brain–computer interface and design... All of this is fascinating, but I'm curious about what it is, specifically, that we're discussing. I find it difficult, if not very hard, to agree or disagree upon anything as long as I remain unsure of that."

Astrid sighed loudly enough for everyone in the room to hear.

Ghaner glanced around, curious and eager for someone to step in and clarify the project he had brought to life.

Yet, no one moved or responded, leaving an uncomfortable silence hanging in the air.

"Well, Thanks, Howard," said Ghaner, before clearing his throat. "As mentioned earlier this week, this event brings together some of the brightest minds to discuss how technological development shapes and curates our experience of the world. Each person here is working on different topics, you're right about that. However, it seems to me that we're all connected in our goal to think critically about these advancements. The premise is the following: technology and digital devices can directly or subliminally influence our minds, and we must be wary of their aims and agendas."

The computer voice echoed: "I'm still a little unsure what we're supposed to do with that."

With a swift motion, Astrid grabbed the microphone and said aloud: "What's unclear, exactly? That we need collaborations and conversations to better design and regulate our future? That expertise should be shared and crossed over to help us regulate our technocratic world? What's so incomprehensibly difficult to grasp?"

The participants stared at her, taken aback by her ferocity.

The voice from the computer chimed in again: "Astrid, this is not how scientific development or scientific criticism works. We would need one clear case study to discuss and understand the object we're dealing with. Not a myriad of experts and opinions laid out, just like that."

Astrid replied, her tone equally compelling: "Well, my dear... this is perhaps why academia and law have failed us so far. Focusing on one object of study at a time... it takes ages to comprehend what companies and corporations are doing in the blink of an eye. If scientific and social frameworks could truly save anything in this world, they would have already done so. This kind of experiment and meet-up might not perfectly work out, that's true, but do you see a feasible alternative? Do you have anything in mind?"

Ghaner glanced at Astrid, a mix of appreciation for her defense and unease about the conversation's unfolding direction.

Jorly, tense, stared at the team of reporters who stared back at her, so much so that one finally found the courage to break the silence: "As you may or may not know, our role is to gather information and present it in a way that enhances public understanding, clearer and more focused. Not everything needs to be perfectly interconnected at this stage. That being said, it would surely be helpful if any of you could speak up whenever you feel the need or urge to address specific concerns related to your research. This way, it will be easier to discuss topics, build consensus, and navigate areas of discord in due time."

Max glanced at Amos and Elena, who sat across the table, seemingly more distracted by the room's temperature than by anything else, endlessly requesting glasses of water from the nearby hostess.

Jona, seated next to her, leaned in and whispered in Max's ear, "Have you ever heard of heat rage?"

"What's that?"

"Extreme heat can create tensions and affect people in some pretty unpleasant ways, both mentally and physically."

Max scanned the crowd.

"I have a suggestion", Klara claimed suddenly.

"Please," validated Ghaner.

"It might be a bit early for us to clearly state what we agree or disagree on..." stated Klara. "For future discussions, I propose the following: after each presentation, we should all identify and document key points of interest, value, and concern. Ideally, by the end of the week, we can deliberate on these collectively or, if necessary, resolve them through a vote."

Seduced by the prospect of an easy and peaceful agreement, the participants began to gently clap.

Max looked again at the leaflet still lying to her right. *Dual Resolve* appeared as an ironic choice of words for a concept that could, perhaps, never work out.

All Max could see was a restless mass of bodies, caught up in the intricacies of the mind, as sweat and ideas flowed through the finest pipelines. She rendered a scene where she was walking through the debate room, now transformed into a forensic zone with dimmed lights. As she slowly pushed the heavy door, it creaked open, revealing the space exactly as it had been left, cluttered with scattered papers and notes.

Yet, the space itself had shifted. The once familiar walls were now lined with thousands of screens and cameras, all flickering with the distant gaze of an invisible crowd. On the far corner of the round table, a shiny and small object caught Max's attention. As she came closer, she recognized her knife, softly gleaming under the cold light.

Max froze, her breath caught in her throat.

She hesitated, torn between the urge to reclaim the object and the fear of being filmed or recognized. In a moment of desperation, she tore a piece from the curtain and wrapped it tightly around her torso and face, concealing herself in its shadowy folds. Now disguised as a strange, almost faceless figure, she advanced toward the table. As her hand closed around the knife, a voice shattered the ominous silence

“I knew it’d be you. I knew it all the time.”

“Max, do you have any ideas or suggestions, perhaps?” Ghaner’s voice snapped Max out of her reverie.

Every member stared at her, anticipating her revelations and insights. But Max knew she couldn’t risk saying something completely off-topic, not with all eyes fixed on her, waiting for a spark of clarity she could not provide.

“I’m sorry,” Max whispered, “I need to go to the bathroom,” before politely heading out.

Murmurs and whispers accompanied her as she walked away.

Ilo, sitting near the exit, watched her leave the room and muttered, “Take this,” handing her a small piece of paper with a note attached.

10.

Drenched in sweat, Max hurried down the corridor. The pervasive heat seemed to choke her. It followed her from the meeting room to every possible corner of the building, leaving little to no space left to breathe.

Arriving in her room and having locked the door behind her, she quickly opened the piece of paper Ilo had given her. Written in a timid, trembling yet pronounced handwriting, Max read: “Tomorrow. 07:00 AM, Seed Vault.”

She pressed the piece of paper in her wet hand. The idea of another excursion with Ilo comforted her, healed by the prospect of deep, fresh, and clear outdoor inhaling. Perhaps, this time, she could sleep.

Lying down, on the verge of sleep, a dream vision took shape: Ilo and her, side by side in bed, surrendering to the heat and the low hum of the pipes, both unafraid, both armed, Max with her knife, Ilo with a gun resting in her left arm.

Max was startled by three sharp knocks.

Nervous, she got up and opened the door, only to discover Elena's fixed gaze. Max tried to push her back, not to let her in, but she could not move any of her body parts. As Elena's figure drew closer, Max somehow succeeded in reaching the knife from under the bed, and pointed it toward Elena.

Slowly, Elena began delicately tracing the edges of the knife with her tongue. It was too gentle to be kind.

Piercing into Max's eyes, Elena whispered, "Why are you only half there? You should behave like a wholeness. Take this blade out of my sight."

***

At 07:00 AM, in the silence of the early morning, Max hurried downstairs, bundled up tightly in layers of clothes.

Ilo was already there, waiting by the airlock door. Like last time, the same choreography played out, yet this time it happened silently. Ilo picked up a gun, entered the password, and offered Max a pair of gloves. Once again, Ilo touched her icy hands, but this time, Ilo did not say a word.

Together, they opened the front door. Max felt courage and pride, as if they were leaving for good. The cold air sliced through her lungs, causing her to pause for a moment before venturing out.

"Shall we?" Ilo's voice felt like warm breath over an icy landscape.

Shivering, Max remained quiet. Her hands clung to the frosted, gurgling banister; she descended the forum steps into the ice-montage.

They made their way toward the Seed Vault, only accompanied by the sound of their footsteps on the ice-covered path.

Each breath cut through Max's lungs. In her pocket, she

held her knife tightly. Yet, she felt foolish for ever assuming there would be any danger nearby.

Ilo walked peacefully and confidently by her side, as if Ilo knew something that everyone else did not, as if she held a treasure that no one ever had.

Slowly, Max could decipher the contours of the Seed Vault, imitating a piece of rock mixed with modern design. The entrance, with its angular structure that emerged from the mountain, felt like the straightest road to nowhere, standing still in the ocean of snow and ice. The blue and grey installation covering the roof reflected the rare glimpses of light and life that abided on Svalbard.

"The Seed Vault... A side gig?" asked Max.

"Sometimes," Ilo retorted. "When other engineers aren't around, they send me here for quick repairs and maintenance."

"How is it inside?"

"How do you imagine a Doomsday Vault?"

"I have nothing coming to mind."

"Lots of tunnels. Thousands of boxes. It looks more exciting from the outside."

Max and Ilo slowly approached the door of the Vault.

"Why here?" whispered Max.

"Above sea level. Implemented within the mountain. Nature's safest guard."

Max and Ilo both stared at the glowing blue building, which was the only trace of light and life in the surrounding landscape.

Max looked at Ilo in silence, her features illuminated by the blue light, the wrinkles of her face becoming more pronounced.

"Will we get in?" wondered Max.

"No, we cannot," replied Ilo sharply.

“So that’s it? And we don't even get to see what's inside?”
“No, but I have something for you.”
Ilo handed another piece of paper to Max.
Her hands trembled, fingers stiff and uncooperative. The carefully wrapped giftpaper warped in her grasp before tumbling into the snow. The black stone sank into the soft, snowy ice. Max quickly bent down to recover the gift.
“I’m sorry...” she mumbled, “I guess the stone is baptized now.”
Ilo laughed. “It’s not a stone. It’s a frozen bud from the Vault.”
Max stared at the dark and shapeless object, which resembled more of a polished stone than something that could be fertilized.
On the piece of paper, Ilo had written the following lines:

Of course, it hurts when buds burst.
Otherwise why would spring hesitate?
Why would all our fervent longing
be bound in the frozen bitter haze?
The bud was the casing all winter.
What is this new thing, which consumes and bursts?
Of course, it hurts when buds burst,
pain for that which grows
and for that which envelops...

“It’s beautiful,” said Max breathily. “Did you write this?”
“I did not,” answered Ilo. “It’s an extract from one of my favorite poems written by Karin Boye.”
“What is it about?”
“A world that fears to exist, afraid of being fulfilled.”
Max smiled as she put the bud and the paper in her pocket.

At that moment, when Max was going to turn away, Ilo whispered: "Can I kiss you?"

The last time Max had kissed someone was on a conventional, busy street, somewhere around the center of Vienna. It happened at the intersection of a McDonald's and a WeekDay, under the perfect cinematographic late-stage capitalistic neon lights. Then, she had faced the realization of her body not responding to the skin of a new lover, the absence of love and warmth. There was nothing scarier than realizing the numbness and the void she had fallen into. It had made her feel beyond empty, clueless about what her body and presence were meant for.

This time, it was different. Ilo's kiss felt like the safest vault for Max's frozen lips, the ultimate place on earth. This time, the light of the Seed Vault was the only source shining onto Ilo's face, and the calmness in the air was the only witness to its charms.

Sensing Ilo was the impossible door to pass through, the one that led from fantasy to reality, the moment when the airlock door finally opened, a move Max would never have made herself.

Ilo was no longer just a concept; she had a texture, a smell, and warmth. Ilo had become a body of flesh, not solely a fantasy or an interface.

In that brief instant, Max forgot about the endless days when she had been unable to care, and the closed-off world in which she had locked herself.

"I could die now," she thought, holding Ilo's cheeks in one hand and her knife in the other.

Ending the kiss, Ilo stared at Max for a while. "Are you feeling okay?"

"Yes," claimed Max. "I just need time."

***

Max stormed into her room and flopped onto the bed, lying flat. The sensation of romance bore a striking resemblance to the fear of waking in the middle of the night, hearing a crack, and reaching for her knife. Desiring felt disturbingly like terror; it had a similar smell and sent the same uncomfortable rush of adrenaline, stress, and survival.

For Max, tales of desire and their possibilities never lasted long: it was a trick she had seen before. Sooner or later, she always ended up at the same point, disappointing the person who loved her as she slowly retreated into the abysses of her mind.

Yet, nothing else truly mattered; the sensation of love and fear intertwined in a dizzying embrace, more real and intense than anything she had ever experienced. Max closed her eyes, a thrill rushing through her, while she wrestled with navigating the moment.

By the time she finally got out of the spiral, it was already past 9:00 AM. She rushed into the shower and threw on the first clothes she found to attend the meeting with Ghaner that she had agreed to.

She passed through the main lounge where breakfast was held, brushing past Elena, who was talking to Klara next to her, and Astrid, seated nearby.

"So, Astrid, tell us," queried Klara," Is desire a fantasy that should never be realized? Does it get its salvation through the body, or only through the mind?"

Max slowed down, eager to hear what she would answer.

Astrid glared back at them with a mix of confusion, as if caught off guard by the irony and absurdity of the question.

In a more typical setting, she would have dismissed

such an affront, but noticing the other guests leaning in, she crafted: “Well, it would be simplistic to claim that desires are merely mental states. I would argue that desires begin in the mind but must extend into other bodily realms. Even if desire is always about the possibility of action instead of the action itself, it is not desirable to separate it from the body. Feeding and nurturing fantasies or fabrications without any real experiences can only lead to despair, or worse, hatred toward real, palpable beings and things. Also, towards life.”

11.

When Max reached Ghaner's door, she knocked twice. She had vivid visions of what his office might be like: a spacious, open environment where creativity could thrive, a place for the master architect to orchestrate ideas. For an intellectual of that caliber, she had imagined a large, round window with a view of the open sky, a clear desk, and tones of yellow and beige to create a lighter atmosphere, layers of books, and various mind maps.

Yet, as Ghaner opened the door, he revealed a narrow, elongated room that looked like a slender, towering structure, hastily constructed and crammed into the space. The faint white light came from a single light source, and his desk, hidden in the shadow, was framed by a chaotic mess cluttered with piles of paperwork.

It was clear that Ghaner had attempted to transform this space, one that wasn't his and never would be, into a small refuge for his thoughts and solace. The walls were bare, devoid of posters or paintings, except for one solitary image tucked away in the corner to his right, held in place by a black pin. The picture, reminiscent of an illustration from an ancient book, depicted two heads adorned with intricate mechanical designs. Both figures gazed toward the past, with the character on the right, seizing a pen in his hand as if inscribing something profound into the other character's mind.

When Ghaner sat down, he paused in silence while gazing at Max.

"So, Max. Where will you return to after this event?"

"Probably back to Vienna."

"Vienna," Ghaner sighed. "A peculiar city... One with a very unique relationship to death, right? What's there, if I may ask?"

"Rent-controlled apartments, cheap university fees, and a fairly decent intellectual scene. Some friends, and mostly, time."

"Time, yes, time. And look at us... and this brief moment we have here. I hope we make the most of it." He paused. "How has it been for you, so far?"

"You know you're on the right path when you start meeting your heroes," answered Max politely.

Ghaner chuckled. "But isn't it also true that it's best never to meet them?"

Max was not sure how to respond.

Ghaner continued: "I've read your book. I think it's fascinating. I wonder how we could find a place or opportunity that aligns with your research and brilliant mind. Perhaps I can assist."

"How?"

"Everything is still to be defined," Ghaner said, as if thinking aloud. "Are you thinking of doing a post-doc, perhaps?"

"I'm not exactly certain about that."

"Yeah. I'd say, think about it twice," Ghaner answered with the hint of a smile. "As you may know... working with academics... And, I can tell you that for a fact..." he continued, "They're annoying. Terrible with time management. Usually can't agree on anything, and more often than not, don't have money. Anyway, Jorly and I plan on organizing more events like this one. Perhaps even creating a center for ethics, somewhere in California. I wish we could be around Europe, but it seems that... they're not yet interested in that. If we start something, anything, I could think of bringing you on board if you'd like that."

Max shook her head. "I'm not entirely sure what I will do next. Perhaps I need to take a break for some time."

Ghaner's eyes flashed. He was intrigued. "Of course. I get it. It can become pretty unhealthy if you only remain active in these areas. But... Perhaps consider it before the offer draws out."

Max frowned at Ghaner. He was smiling, yet Max noticed a hint of despair and fear in his eyes. He seemed to be crying out for warmth and care.

In stark contrast, and in that precise moment, Max knew she radiated confidence; no hint of uncertainty ever seemed to penetrate her.

In a flash, he rose from his chair and closed the distance to Max. He seized her hand, making her flinch in surprise.

He placed Max's hand over his heart and laughed.

"Can you feel this?" Ghaner asked. "Funny thing is, I'm already enhanced!"

He laughed again. "The mind is a remarkable place to inhabit, and I surely agree with that. But without my pacemaker, I wouldn't be here. Perhaps, in the end, one needs the body too."

Max smoothly removed her hand and got up to leave.

"Sorry, I need to rehearse for this morning's presentation."

Her gaze was unsettled, and her cheeks were blushing. When she left the room, she rushed to the bathroom to sit in silence. In reality, there was nothing to rehearse. Max knew her topic by heart. Presenting her research was, rather simply, to display her life. Fear had long since left her; public speaking was now second nature, and her hands no longer trembled in front of an audience. There was something melancholic about her ease, a jaded indifference that she had mastered over time, even when the subject was so intimately tied to her mind.

***

At 10:00 AM, Max walked onto the stage, the blinding lights dancing at the edge of her vision, momentarily disorienting her. The surroundings blurred into vague shapes, the audience became mere silhouettes, their figures merging and shedding their skins as they settled into their seats.

Max, unsettled by the scene, searched for a focal point, her eyes finally landing on the water bottle on her right side. She caught a glimpse of Ilo's face, a brief flicker of warmth softening her heart and gaze.

A voice emerged behind her, and Max, startled, softly jumped in her chair, nearly toppled by the technician.

"Are you ok?" asked the young man. "This is your mic."

"Yeah, thanks. I'm fine."

Before Max had a chance to speak, Bill, who was the designated moderator, appeared on stage. With ease and comfort, seemingly unfazed by the condensed air or the gazes fixed upon him, he declared: "We're honored to welcome Max, who, as you may have noticed, is one of our youngest speakers. It's a real pleasure to have her on stage, as her research offers a remarkable contribution to the themes we're exploring this week here in Svalbard."

Max slowly turned around, facing the immense projection and title of a book she was not sure anymore she had herself birthed: *Easy To Hate: The Imperfect Body in the Technological Turn*. The collection of words reminded her of an era of her life that she often wished to turn into a blackout.

Still unable to fully grasp the scene unfolding in front of her, Max smiled in confusion at the blurry spectacle of lights. Before she had a chance to take another sip of water to refresh her already dry mouth, the audience began to applaud.

The air cleared up a bit, and she could start to discern a few familiar faces. Sitting there, under the spotlight of the public's piercing gazes and their applause, Max revisited the first time her book was publicly released.

On that particular evening, a new experience was unlocked. In a joyful setting where visitors endlessly congratulated her, Max had felt an enormous emptiness, a profound sense of despair. Amid success, signing books, hugging, and laughing with anyone who came around, she couldn't help but think of all the people who had once been there, loved her, but left her because of who she was.

She recalled her retreat from the world and from experience. The many times she wished she didn't have a body, the pain of being with others and disappointing them, the times reality fell short of her fantasies, the lovers she had lied to, the performances she had put on. She remembered the empty, cold beds, the bruises, the impossibility of touch at night. Right now, while facing the small crowd and the cameras, Max could only acknowledge her failures.

Still, she recited the lines she had come to know so intimately into the microphone, carried back to the pain and loss that had driven her to write. While moving from one quote to another, one slide to another, she relived the profound loneliness that accompanied her throughout. Amid that solitude, writing had become an essential lifeline.

Yet, sitting here, lecturing others about a book that had mostly brought her pain, she no longer knew for whom she was doing all of this. While reciting her dry and soulless text, Max dwelled upon the mere existence of pride, recognition, and pleasures, where and how to find them. Speaking without even feeling the words, and with teary eyes, Max ended with a dry "Thank you" before putting the microphone down.

When the applause was finally over, Max turned around and walked off the stage.

Bill stopped her, grabbing her by the shoulder: "Wait, Max, wait. I'm sure the audience has many questions or remarks for you. Can you sit back?"

Dizzy and half-unaware, Max slid back.

The performance had felt like watching herself from the outside. "Can I get... a glass... refill," she murmured mechanically.

The microphone already moved swiftly through the crowd.

"Thanks for this presentation," claimed a stranger's voice. "Don't you think that dismissing the body stems from a high-end elite perspective that often overlooks one's privilege? Who can truly afford not to think about the body? Ultimately, isn't mind enhancement an issue that's unlikely to become widely globalized? Perhaps it is time for all of us here to touch grass."

Max, unable to discern the speaker's face, focused on his voice.

Her memory snapped back.

The sharp, confrontational remark had come from Francis Kolman, a philosopher she had met during a symposium at NYU Steinhardt. She vividly recalled his conceited presence and his pompous gestures: how he barely made eye contact as he handed her a USB drive, explaining his latest efforts to create an alternative physical pirate library. Francis had suggested that Max upload her new research onto the USB for wider distribution. She responded with a polite yet bitter smile and said: "I'll do it."

Both of them knew it was a lie.

To Max, Francis Kolman was yet another middle-aged man presenting the idealistic vision of a critical open-source utopia. He was the type who yearned *to touch grass*, to connect with the tangible world outside the digital realm, and yet, paradoxically, he seemed unable to do so, for he was not fully aware of his own privileges in the spaces he traversed. In this domain, such performative Marxist middle-aged men existed in abundance, but none had offered to pay Max's bills, hire her for a research position, or share any sort of benefits.

Shaking off the memory, Max gathered her thoughts, took hold of the microphone, and uttered in response: "Indeed, we seemed to all be privileged here. Yet, I do not believe that kids who are addicted to video games, individuals falling in love with AIs, or teenagers experiencing internet-related body dysmorphia are specifically entitled. My research solely builds on virtual phenomena to render how, in these experiences, the body is often rendered as a failure, an obstacle to the desires of the mind. To discuss this mere desire, and the ways it is being utilized, capitalized, and harvested by and through technology, is the consideration we're working on here, am I right?"

Kolman remained quiet, not responding with any of his usual remarks.

Bill started clapping first. The rest of the crowd followed slowly, then more assuredly.

"Anyone? Any questions?" asked Bill as Max tried to get up, out of sight.

In the corner, close to the exit, Ilo stood quietly against the wall.

"Well done, Miss Enhancement."

At the sight of Ilo miming, Max's lips curved into a smile. Yet, she longed for everything to be different.

12.

The following night, sleep had become an elusive reality, slipping through Max's hands with each passing hour. The relentless clanking and hissing of the pipes, fused with her racing thoughts and intertwined with the mounting anxiety that social gatherings and forced conversations gave her, were etched into her soul.

She felt drained, her energy sapped by the weight of interactions and expectations that demanded more than she could give.

In the room, the air had grown nearly unbreathable. Max frantically stuffed the pipes entering and exiting the room with some of her clothes, hoping to halt the airflow.

Yet, this attempt to suffocate the building felt disturbingly akin to a tragic act of self-harm.

Overcome by the futility of it all, Max gave up. She collapsed onto the ground in a wave of despair, her body wracking with soft cries.

She left her room, hoping to find relief elsewhere, closer to Ilo's room and the engine controlling the heat forecast. As she found herself in front of Ilo's door, Max knocked three times, each rap of her knuckles against the wood a plea for solace.

When Ilo opened the door, there was little surprise in her eyes, and for Max, stepping into this room felt like sliding the final piece into a long-troubling puzzle, the hidden key to an escape game that had held her captive for far too long. She inhaled deeply, savoring the fresh air. Her body began to unwind.

"You seem discouraged," remarked Ilo, dryly.

"Perhaps what technology offered to us is something we do not deserve, and should not have."

"What shouldn't we have?"

"Control over experiences. Agency over facts. Fantasies over reality. All of the things we've been speculating about."

The silence occupied the space for a little while.

"Why did you reach my room this time?"

"I couldn't breathe in mine."

Max glanced at Ilo and quickly looked away, gesturing toward the piles of books next to the bed. Her eyes settled on one title she recognized: *Neige Noir*.

"Can you read French?"

Her curiosity was piqued by the familiar name.

"A little bit. I learned during an exchange program a few years ago. Trying to keep up with it."

Max reached for the book and read the back cover.

"Is this book about Svalbard?"

"Yes, partly."

"Are you doing site-specific readings?"

"A friend recommended it to me when she heard I'd be based here for a short while. I like it. It's a mix of theater, novel, and script... confusing but good, somehow."

"What's the plot?"

Ilo laughed while handing Max one of the two small mugs of sleeping tea.

"Two lovers go to Svalbard for their honeymoon, but then the fiancé dies. At first, it appears to be a suicide, but then it gets blurry, and we start to suspect that it might be a murder orchestrated by the narrator. It's rather unclear, as the story seems to unfold based on the main character's decisions. As if he could precisely choose what happens and what is designed, reshuffling the storyline at will, shaping it to his desire."

"Stressful." Max sat down on the sofa.

"It is. I also found out that the author, Hubert Aquin, killed himself. But there's this one quote I like."

Max eyed Ilo as she skimmed through the pages.

When Ilo found the quote, she whispered: "Love gives vertigo, but its dizziness, as intolerable as it may be, is an infinite delight."

Max grinned, unsure where to look.

Ilo's smile lingered as she looked up from the book, a quiet confidence in her gaze. She took another sip from her cup, then slowly sat closer. Ilo's elbow touched Max's arm.

They both whispered, "Sorry."

"Do you want to sleep here?"

"I think, I want to, yes."

Ilo prepared the bed, changed, and invited Max to join her. They both lay down at opposite ends of the bed, seemingly avoiding any accidental contact. Despite the warmth and safety of Ilo's body, Max remained too awake and alert to doze off. She was in her bed.

She whispered: "Could you tell me a story?"

"A story?"

"I don't think I can fall asleep just like this."

Ilo laughed.

"What do you want?"

"A quote, an anecdote, whatever comes to mind."

"I know this might sound cliche, but..."

Ilo turned around and began expressing her fascination with Leonardo da Vinci. Her voice carried a blend of admiration and curiosity, recounting anecdotes and trivia about his life and works. Max could hear in the tone of Ilo's voice the value she placed on his accomplishments, his relationships with both men and women, the ambiguity of his attractions, and the mysteries surrounding his life.

"His grandfather would often tell him, 'Po l'occhio', encouraging Leonardo to pay attention to the surrounding nature," whispered Ilo while looking at the ceiling's soft light.

"I'm always trying to do a little bit of that."

Cradled by the soft and healing tones of Ilo's voice, Max gradually drifted into the depths of Morpheus's realm.

A second later, Max found herself back in the same room, the same bed, yet the colors of the walls had changed. Ilo was still lying down and speaking, but in a language that Max couldn't quite understand.

Max turned her way, finding Ilo staring back at her. Ilo's face was different, her body distorted, yet her voice was intact. Max drew near her quietly and kissed her, slowly at first, and within the next seconds, Ilo grasped Max's body to bring her closer. The soft humidity of the room imprinted on their skins, and as they made out, a selection of random words surfaced.

When Max opened her eyes, Ilo was still there, facing the wall, softly speaking.

Their bodies weren't touching, and the ocean between their flesh remained infinite.

Max was thinking of acting upon the feeling of lust, of shifting the dream into reality, but there was something about the air of this room, of the one she was actually in, that did not leave her the opportunity to become an actor on this stage.

Max observed Ilo, pondering why on earth she couldn't make a move and wondering if Ilo knew what she had seen.

Frozen and still unable to move, Max slowly faded out again.

Back in the strangely rendered room, Max and Ilo's bodies were, once again, linked together.

In a desperate attempt to enact, and fully conscious of the nature of such a lucid dream, Max caught Ilo's lips and started kissing her again, slowly escalating and moving down her body. Ilo's movements and ease left Max perplexed. It seemed so soft, so easy to be inhabited in such skin. Slowly, they started caressing each other. Each of their hands was preoccupied with touching every possible part of the other's naked body. Wet and warm, the two bodies merged into one, forever glued in a moment that did not fully exist.

Max woke up again.

Ilo, on her side, was fully asleep.

Max, still reeling from the dream, thought of all the possible ways, all the potential strength she needed to summon to dare to touch Ilo's skin. The dream had felt so soft, so pleasurable, and the reality of the room she found herself in was too tangible, too concrete, somewhat unreal. Max fought to muster the will to transpose the moment she had felt in the dream into what she believed was real, but Morpheus's grasp was too strong, and the allure of a room that Ilo would never know about was far too enticing.

When she drifted again, Ilo was on top of her. The pleasure had never been so firm, so intense. It was different from everything Max knew, a far stretch from the consciousness of the body, from the limitations of the flesh; it was erotica subjectively and intuitively rendered, the epitome of all erotic dreams.

Max was too clueless, too intoxicated to deny her desire, fully conscious of the lucid nature of this journey. She merged even deeper into the layers of her lover's skin. Max was on the verge, too close to climax, but never quite reaching it.

She wondered if this was the moment, perhaps even the sign, to wake up and finally touch Ilo, for real, knowing that nothing might ever feel as good as the dream.

Conscious again, Max found her own body warm, suffocated, and wet.

Ilo was still sleeping, unaware of the entire journey her projected body had been on. In the room, there was no tension, no smell of care or traces of lust. The warmth of Max's body and the very recent memory of arousal were too beautiful, too naive, too intense to be left untouched.

Max allowed herself to slide back into the soft dream where she knew Ilo was waiting for her, wet and soft, where nothing needed to be explained, no foreplay needed to be installed, and where instant pleasures just manifesed. There, Ilo's body had no textures or smell; it was only a vessel for what Max's mind commanded.

Back in Ilo's arms, Max recognized the golden color of what it felt like to be loved, to be fucked, and in that awakening experience, she imagined, for a second, that this was perhaps what it felt like to be touched by God. The subtle changes in movement and the elasticity of their skin, made both of them reach a climax, a dream-rendered pleasure that could make one forever regret the limitations of reality.

When Max woke up, Ilo was still sleeping.

No closure had been given, and no intimacy was experienced.

A single tear dropped from Max's eyes. Once again, she had failed to act upon her dreams.

Hours later, when Ilo eventually woke up, she noticed Max's strange distance.

"Are you okay?"

Max supposed for a moment the outcomes of telling Ilo about her dream. A part of her wanted Ilo to know that she loved her and that something great had happened. Another part feared that Ilo wouldn't understand.

"Nothing," whispered Max. "I dreamed of you."

"How was it?"

"I'm sorry," said Max, while dressing up. "I don't remember."

***

Walking toward the dorms, Max replayed the haunting, soft, and dreamy memories of the night before, unsure where to store them in her mind.

Passing through the second lounge, she noticed one of the reporters sitting alone at the corner of the bar.

He looked dejected, defeated, and lost.

Without a proper thought, Max sat down beside him.

"May I?" she asked.

"Of course," he replied with a short sigh.

The bartender asked if Max wanted a drink.

Max stared at her watch. It was not even nine.

"No," she said. "Not in the morning."

"I'm drinking a soft," the reporter retorted.

Feeling foolish for projecting a despair that didn't quite match the situation, Max sat in silence for a while.

"It's confusing, isn't it?"

"A little bit," answered the reporter while drinking from his glass. "But I've seen worse, to be honest."

"Worse? I'd love to see that."

"Trust me, you wouldn't. Scientists, thinkers, and politicians throwing jabs at each other, no one's listening, nothing's happening, just brags."

"What's different with what is going on here?"

"This time, it's something I personally care about."

"So what's with the face?" asked Max.

The reporter fell silent, glancing around to make sure no one could overhear. Then, hesitantly, he spoke up.

"Jorly. She's making things... difficult. But hey, she's the one paying for all of that."

"Difficult?"

"She and the other investors demand clearer, more defined results from this event, but they also do not want anything overly critical."

"What is she asking then?"

"It's not Jorly, directly. It's the ecosystem around her. She's been hinting that we could... rewrite the report," he paused, "but I mean, it makes sense. It's not just Jorly and Ghaner involved, neither you nor I. She has too many important connections. If the report isn't supporting what her peers are doing or developing... She'd run into problems."

"Problems?"

"Well, as you might know, these people aren't exactly fans of critical thinking, and even less of the possibility of ethics," he continued. "They support it, yes, from a philosophical standpoint. But they prefer it to stay within that intellectual realm. Once ethics turn into laws and regulations, progress slows down."

"But if everything's recorded, there's no way to fudge what has been said or discussed, right?"

"Well, we all signed an NDA, but nothing is going live. God knows what they will publish in the aftermath."

He paused, sighed, and concluded: "I don't like to admit this, but the more I attend events like this one, the more they feel like a performance of concern rather than a genuinely revolutionary act."

Max stared silently at the reporter, then she said, "We're all trying our best."

"Yeah," the reporter replied, raising his glass as if to toast. "Let's hope it's enough."

13.

When Max decided to get up from her chair, leaving the reporter at the bar, an intense, unshakable tension coiled within her legs and arms. Her body ached with a deep, persistent soreness that she could not justify. The feeling, though, wasn't unknown.

She pulled up her pant leg and rolled back her sleeve, only to discover that the bruises had intensified. With no place to hide, Max rushed to her room to lie down for a little while. Fighting against the anger and the spasms, Ilo's sweet image returned to her mind. Max sensed within herself the birth of a burning desire. A heat she had often seen in others, a fuel for touch and for desire. Something that she wasn't sure she was even capable of.

Max dissected Ilo's image. Her magical nature. Her playful gaze. Her sensual and energetic thrive. Everything Max loved and desired, yet could not materialize. Memories of Ilo seemed to soothe her momentarily, yet, at the same time, they were a reminder of a disillusionment she knew too well: the rise and fall of her hopes and her desires. How many times would this cycle repeat? What could be different this time?

Softly suffocating, sweating, and choking on her twisted memories, Max decided to get out of the room.

She began pacing the lounge in circles like a desperate animal. In the midst of one of these restless laps, her thoughts consumed and her steps quickening, she walked into Amos, who was passing by.

"Are you okay?" he asked, his voice tinged with genuine worry.

Max paused, the question hanging in the air before she responded, her voice trembling slightly.

"You have a gun license, right?"

He nodded slowly.

Max started walking toward the airlock, Amos following her close behind.

Amos entered the password for the locker where the guns were stored.

Max scrutinized his gestures. By then, she had seen the combinations of numbers three times.

As they walked out of the Science Center, embracing the deadly wind of Svalbard, Amos asked what their destination was.

Max kept quiet. Amos followed her patiently toward the end of a nearby street, struggling to navigate the layers of ice. After trudging through a few hundred meters of snow, they arrived.

Max pushed with all her strength.

The heavy wooden door opened with one hand.

"A bar?" asked Amos.

Inside, the interior evoked the cozy charm of a ski lodge, with warm wood accents and soft candlelight. Amos settled into a corner of the bar, while Max took the seat across from him.

The bartender came their way with quiet warmth.

"What can I serve you?"

"Do you have Baileys?"

"Oh, my... That's a sweet tooth we have here."

"One big glass, please," she requested, "with lots of piled ice."

"Is it not cold enough outside for your taste?" The bartender chuckled.

"Just enough, yes," she replied, smiling coldly.

***

By 11:30 AM, Max had ordered her fourth glass.

The pain was finally dissolving into the sweet, caramelized abyss.

Amos had said nothing.

When Max closed her eyes, there was nowhere to wander except Ilo's enigmatic smile.

"A world that fears to exist, afraid of being fulfilled," she recalled.

When she ordered her fifth glass, the bartender approached her, his expression tinged with concern.

"My dear, perhaps you should slow down."

"I'm not going to pass out here just by drinking fucking Bailey's, don't worry."

"Yes. Better not die!"

Amos looked at the bartender, concerned about the gravity of his remark.

The bartender returned his gaze: "Don't know the joke? It's illegal to decay here."

Max looked up like a drunken man who had heard a funny and uncanny line.

The bartender laughed. “There is this saying... ‘No one births or dies in Svalbard.’”

“I can do what the fuck I want...” whispered Max.

“It’s not about you,” paused the bartender. “We simply cannot leave dead bodies on the island. In the cold, bodies don’t decompose well, and in the worst case, the cold keeps viruses frozen in the skin layers, which could be dangerous for the island’s ecosystem.”

“What if there is an accident?” pondered Amos.

“Well, for those who unfortunately pass away before they can move to the mainland, cremation is the only choice,” answered the bartender. “But it requires getting a state license for cremation and burying the urn, which can be a long and bureaucratic process... All in all, it’s best to avoid confronting death while you’re here.”

Gazing into the melted chocolate-like appearance of her glass, Max retreated into her thoughts.

Even though Ilo seemed like the sweetest escape route toward another life, there was nothing Max could propose. She had no vision for her future, no place where she had ever truly settled, nothing she was truly proud of. Max wished she had a more concrete plan, a more tangible life, one with warmth and a home, but she had none of that. Back home, Max’s daily life resembled that of a maniacal researcher obsessed with concepts rather than a life open to loving another human. Her habits as an introverted thinker and library rat, though impressive to her peers, were often too unsexy and unappealing for a long-term romantic life.

“How does it feel to live so far from everything?” pondered Amos, breaking into Max’s daydreams.

"I grew into it," the bartender replied.

"You never feel like you're missing out?"

"Missing out on what? The delirium and fast-paced and despairful society?" chuckled the bartender. "I don't. I like the idea of contemplating the world from afar. It's most often better heard or read about. There are too many things and confusion going on everywhere. I wouldn't give up this state of mind and this view of the world."

"Doesn't it get lonely?"

"Certainly, but wherever one wanders, one cannot escape oneself."

Max stared at the other corner of the bar, listening carefully. Everywhere she went, she saw herself. There was nowhere she could hide. Even an iced island on the other side of the world reminded her of that.

***

By the time Max had finished her eighth glass, she glanced at the clock on the wall. It could have been 2:00 or 10:00, 6:00 or 9:00. No daylight could reveal this information. As she tried to stand up, she fell back and hit the corner of her ribcage.

"Wow, slow down. You need to eat something before doing anything else," said the bartender, placing a piece of bread in front of Max.

"Ok, enough," said Amos, who paid quickly and grabbed Max by the arm, dragging her outside.

The bartender watched them as they walked away from the bar.

Stumbling awkwardly back toward the Science Center, Max, dizzy from the alcoholic and sugary Baileys, murmured a soft "thanks" to Amos, who carried her to the dorms and gently laid her down in his bed.

Drunkenly lying there, Max closed her eyes, wishing for the Science Center to be consumed by flames, or frozen in time, suspended forever in an unbreakable stillness. She dreamed of nature reclaiming its dominion over the sterile walls, snow drifting through the broken windows, covering the floors, and trees breaking through the pipes.

There, the cameras were the only audience left, silently recording a world in which human constructs had faded away, leaving behind nothing but the raw, untamed forces of nature. Ghaner, Klara, Jorly, and Amos would be chastized by the forces of Earth for what they had wished. For the dream of a place where the physical self either ceased to exist or could be harvested, for a cold, mechanized future where nature was endlessly pursued and endlessly replicated because it could no longer be experienced.

14.

When Max woke up, it was already dinner time. Alone in Amos's small bed, she quickly gathered her things and headed down the corridor toward her own room.

Her legs felt unsteady, her thoughts still tangled in the haze of sleep.

She jumped into the shower. The fabric of her clothes clung to her skin as the water hit her. She had forgotten to undress. With both arms resting against the wall and her head bent low, she turned on the cold water, hoping its shock would jolt her back to full consciousness.

The icy stream ran past her head and mouth, and she thought of the stories she could spin to explain her absence. That she had lost track of time, or simply dozed off. That she had some urgent task online.

Each excuse felt flimsy, disappearing as quickly as the water was swirling down the drain. The truth was even harder to render, slippery, out of reach.

On her way to dinner, she caught the faint echo of a

casual conversation from the conference area. Max crept toward the room, silently trying to identify the voices that echoed and intensified like muffled sounds.

She wanted to know what she might have missed.

As she gradually neared, she recognized the voices of Ghaner, Astrid, and Jorly chatting.

"To me, it does not matter if a consensus is hard to reach. You've heard my point many times. We need stories that go beyond the binary of right and wrong, or good and evil. The fact alone that the report might be complex to write, is no surprise. Still, as we have agreed upon, its quality and usability should remain the focus of our deliverables."

Ghaner remained silent.

Astrid's voice took over: "So that's it? You'd be satisfied with a somewhat realistic, slightly nuanced report? What is such a document going to bring to the table? While you sit here indifferently, I'd rather hold some people and power structures accountable."

"But isn't the attempt alone of displaying so many experts and perspectives already valuable in itself?" asked Ghaner. "This is a first experiment, after all! We're simply attempting to make different worlds collide."

"So what?" replied Astrid with disdain. "You're thinking that by displaying your network and money in events like this one, you're going to save the world from techno dystopias, and additionally wash away the specks of dirt tainted on the cash that made all this silly theater come into life?"

Embarrassed, Ghaner observed Astrid with a tormented gaze, as if subliminally trying to calm her down.

But Astrid wasn't the kind. When it seemed that she was about to go on, he grabbed her by the shoulder, telling Jorly that both of them would go for a smoke in a dedicated room next to the lounge.

"I don't smoke," said Astrid, annoyed by the mentoring aspect of his request, "You know that."

"It does not matter," insisted Ghaner. "I need you to come by."

***

That evening, the dining room was transformed into a luxurious theater decorated with chandeliers and soft lights.

Max moved through the space like a silent specter, a calm yet slightly apprehensive figure treading cautiously. She was among familiar faces, yet she debated whom to approach, finally settling into the first available chair she found.

She exchanged greetings with those who recognized her before focusing her gaze on the empty plate in front of her.

Out of the corner of her eye, she noticed Klara, seemingly comfortable and at ease, laughing at any advances and intellectual queries. Somewhere on the left side, Amos, who did not notice Max's comeback, was sharing his latest findings, vividly arguing for his findings and their consequences.

Max could hear him listing his affiliations with various labs, passionately arguing that cognitive enhancement could thrive not only with brain-computer-interface designs but also with the normalization and legalization of drugs and stimulants.

Jona interjected: "Isn't that interesting? There's hardly any moral discussion surrounding the enhancement of our abilities with external devices, yet there's a vast debate about the ethics of psychopharmaceuticals. What do you make of that?"

“I suppose it’s because one seems more overt than the other,” answered Amos while pouring himself a glass. “Swallowing pills and chemicals suggests direct intrusions of external substances into what we consider to be our lives, which is why it garners so much attention.”

He paused for a moment before continuing. “Psycho-pharmaceuticals are designed to directly alter or improve one’s experience and existence, while enhancement through cognitive technologies can manifest as more... subliminal. Thus, it is so difficult to discuss or mentor over time.”

Unwilling to partake in any of these discussions and unsure where to rest her gaze, Max let her eyes move to the rim of her water glass, its surface shimmering under the soft light. Sitting in silence, she ruminated on the gestures and actions she could take to avoid appearing too disposable or overly eager to join any conversation.

When she finally looked away from her glass, Elena appeared on her right side, standing like a sharp figure emerging from a blurry heat wave.

“Ah, there you are,” she pondered, smiling. “We weren’t sure you’d come.”

“You weren’t?” asked Max.

“Well, you’ve been absent today, am I right?”

Max said nothing and instead stared at the transparent glass.

“Would you like something to drink?”

Max hesitated but knew the night would feel endless if she didn’t join her on that dance. Arriving late and then leaving too early could come across as one more manifestation of her indifference.

Max glanced at Elena from the corner of her eye and noticed, by the way she poured her drink, that she was shaking, perhaps even drunk or high.

"Well, then, tell Max," inquired Elena. "What's the matter?"

"Excuse me?" countered Max, not knowing how to respond to this request.

"I've been watching you the last few days, and I've felt you're... distant. Worried, maybe?"

"I have a lot of work," answered Max while sipping her drink."It sometimes takes over everything else."

"Work? You're getting paid to be here, aren't you?"

"I'm talking about ongoing things. There's a life after Svalbard, right?"

"Say, what a routine you have," said Elena. "Do you ever just... relax?"

Elena raised her glass in the air.

"See if I were still your age... I'd do anything and everything," she continued, "You have the rest of your life to be frigid, cold, and absent-minded."

Max was surprised to find Elena seemingly unable to relate to her reality. After all, she, too, had been disillusioned by life and was now attached to the ghost of a man.

"Look at you... Cute as a button... and turning down opportunities... What are you thinking?" continued Elena.

"That your magnetism is immortal?"

Max did not respond.

"I've seen the way they all look at you. And you know what the worst part is? I get it."

"You do?"

"Shameless," Elena chuckled. "Of course, I do. Look at you, look at me. I'm his wife."

Elena glanced in the direction of Klara.

"Young things like you are a glutton for the mind. But one day, you will certainly be the shadow of someone. And at worst, it'll be a man."

Elena poured herself another glass, swaying away.

"Failure has a peculiar depth," Max said to herself.

But no words left her lips.

The first failure remains a small, secret tale, kept close because it might be mere bad luck or something else. Failing a second, third, or more times tasted like a slow, bitter acknowledgment of reality.

At least, it's easier to fail alone, Max thought.

"But this life isn't bad," Elena had returned. "Imagine: you come home, you own a cat, and your husband arrives in a suit and tie. Your career feels like a long-forgotten dream that, anyway, had no chance to survive. The curated objects in your living room feel just right. Wouldn't you love that?"

Burdened by Elena's cryptic allusions, Max shot back:

"What's your advice, then? Should I steal your man?"

"What a purity of spirit..." Elena laughed cynically. "But I don't buy your story for a second. Why come here? To play the intellectual ghost in the theater of the absurd? You must love this a little bit. Otherwise, you wouldn't have come around."

Max watched Elena, feeling a wave of disgust wash over her.

As Max began to stand up, Elena grabbed her hand.

"Playing frigid works for you now, while you're young and bursting with life. But remember, life might last a little longer than that."

"Failure has a peculiar depth," Max hissed, wishing that Elena understood her side of the story. Once acknowledged, it cannot be unseen. It's this word, once used sparingly, that becomes one's mantra. It's the untold story, the story of others, the narrative of those who wait, proclaiming victimhood, and the poetry of those who pass. It's the desperate act of moving from place to place, audaciously searching for the missing piece of oneself, knowing the same issues will resurface.

Elena was right.

Max could chase fleeting highs, indulge in quick fixes, delve into substances, flirt with every new opportunity, sleep little, write incessantly, feeling somewhat like a rock-star, calling it a life. Alternatively, she had chosen to isolate, reflect, and immerse herself in a sadness that mirrored her life. Naked before Elena's eyes, there were no sanctuaries for Max, no places to hide.

Ghaner watched Elena and Max conversing from afar, his expression marked by worry. He didn't intervene.

Amid the incessant clamor of laughter and insincere praise, Max stayed silent, still lengthening the monologue within her mind. As she finally stood up to leave, she dropped a few final words: "Don't you know... that they don't want this?"

"Humble? You don't seem like the type."

"I've just seen it many times already. Desiring me and leaving me for the same reasons."

"Which are?"

"Fantasies and illusions. Projections and deceptions. Lies."

Elena sighed as if annoyed by Max's insights.

"Remaining distant and afar is also something *you do*. Don't you know that negation feeds desire?"

Max stood up, morbid and silent. Now standing, Max noticed the traces of smoke from microwave-heated food lingering in the air.

As she walked out, she crossed paths with Ilo: "Where

were you today? How did you get out?"

Max ignored her as she strode out.

***

At night, Max revisited her arrival in Svalbard.

Sitting in the shuffle, Ilo was the one driving this time. The landscape of Svalbard was not a frozen wasteland anymore. Instead, it had transformed into a burning and heated land, filled with thousands of flames. In the distance, the Science Center radiated with millions of orange flares and lights.

Max could see the structure of the building bursting and collapsing, accompanied by the frantic screams of guests and other individuals desperately trying to escape. Ilo, at the wheel, gave Max a knowing look and said softly: "Experimental."

15.

The following morning, Max returned to her treadmill, hoping to find solace in the only thing that offered the simulation of another destination.

She started to run.

Whenever the thought of slowing down crossed her mind, she forcefully reminded herself of every moment her body had faltered, the intense physical pain she had endured. She kept running. The ultimate act of punishment.

Max sought to capture the essence of Svalbard in the summer to ignite her relentless drive. In her mind, she drew a painting of an impending spring and imagined that, if she ran fast enough, she might reach this elusive destination, an escape road where healing powers awaited her upon arrival. Yet, these visions were surely but slowly accompanied by the unbearable spasms in her lower abdomen.

With closed eyes, Max breathed heavily and loudly. A few others who were present in the gym paused to watch her. She was gasping like a horse on its last legs, refusing to give up as she exorcised her pain through sweat.

As Klara pushed open the humid door of the gym, she saw Max, her tear-streaked face pale and hollow, her body straining against the treadmill. A lifeless creature caught in motion. Running in her direction, Klara shouted Max's name, trying to get her to stop.

Max did not hear it.

Possessed, she kept on running, pushing through the idea of spring and change. Her feet were glued to the treadmill. She couldn't disconnect nor arrive.

Klara, worried, rushed to the machine to press the emergency button, forcing Max to slow down.

As Max was coming back to consciousness and realized that her performance had become a public spectacle, she rushed out and stumbled toward the restroom to hide and vomit repeatedly.

Letting herself unravel completely, she hoped to emerge cleansed when the purge would be over, her breath heavy against the bare ground of the basement gym in Svalbard.

When she was done, she left the bathroom, lay down on a nearby couch, and fell asleep. In her short-lived nap, the same recurring figure, that of a stranger entering and evading the room, walked toward her. Their shapeless body defined the landscape, but no name, no gaze, called out. She fought to banish the image of the stranger's disguise and tried to remember Ilo's hand as a guide. The stranger pointed in her direction, forcing her to look at her own body.

Max looked at herself: her flesh had been bruised and stabbed a hundred times.

She woke up, as if electrocuted by life.

Drowsy, she headed through the main area, hoping to remain out of sight.

Rushing to her room, she showered quickly and collapsed on the bed, praying to every god and saint she knew that the rest of the day would bring relief, or at least give her the strength to perform.

***

Stationed in the lecture room, hoping it would be the last time, Max struggled to gather her thoughts. She had no desire to sit through another disagreement, another senseless debate, but she couldn't leave just yet.

In the corner of the room, Ilo stood as usual, unperturbed, static, somehow functional, and resigned to every conceivable fact. In the hot air, Max could smell the perfumes of plastic pipelines.

Amos, who was standing proudly on stage, began his speech: "As discussed during the week, new technologies facilitate the enhancement of a wide range of human dispositions, capacities, or abilities. While it is argued that we need to set limits to human enhancement, it is unclear where we should find the resources to set such limits. I am here today, one of the last, to address an ongoing debate which seems to be emerging in the field of bioethics as consideration toward future development and technologies play out."

"One of the last," Max whispered.

An unusual sensation gripped her heart as if she were about to depart without completing something crucial. She, who had come to explore and encounter the future, now found herself devoid of any desire to delve deeper or engage further with the possibilities of the mind.

Max looked around. The guests were sweating and breathing heavily, yet still riveted by Amos, who was, through unknown forces, captivating the attention of the entire crowd.

"Research on brain–computer interface interfaces has primarily been introduced to support individuals with impairments. I must first acknowledge that this focus is well-founded and that the developments in this area have been incredibly positive."

Despite Max's attempt to exhaust herself to the point of collapse on the treadmill, an inexplicable and persistent energetic pain lingered. An irrational blend of intense emotional cocktails brewed from all the terrifying realizations, whether awake or asleep, the past lingered.

Thinking of her bruised body, Max was searching for a culprit, for someone to blame, always, but there were no clear moments or people to pinpoint, no specific individuals to blame, no single entity to condemn. For years already, she had yearned to understand the reasons behind her easily bruised skin, her volatile reactions, the sudden pain and spasms, or her body's reluctance to be touched. But there was no singular, monolithic reason to be found.

If only there were one. She could direct all her anger toward that one source, confront it, and heal somewhat, perhaps.

"I suppose the question that is being addressed throughout these conversations is the following: what could be the difference between therapy and enhancement? When is it a cure, and when is it a curse?"

Max glanced at Ilo, who, miraculously, was also looking in her direction. Max's pale face was worrisome, and yet, Ilo looked caringly upon her, like a gentle caress in a nightmare.

Glued to her chair, Max felt like an animal in a cage that had no legs to escape.

The exit, hovering at the ceiling, accompanied by the positioning of the lights, had formed a portal just above Max's head, a door toward another path.

"Medicinal practices have traditionally focused on the process of healing," Amos argued. "The responsibilities of doctors are defined not just by their knowledge and skills, but by the true essence of healing. However, skeptics argue that the act of enhancing does not equate to healing. Consequently, some believe that enhancement falls outside the scope of medicine."

Max ruminated on everything that happened since her arrival. Her initial excitement. The tickling of endless noises emitting through the pipelines. The insistent gaze of Amos and the constant presence of the knife. The fears and visions that had accompanied her throughout. Ilo's presence, like a fresh breeze, an unexpected glimmer of light amid the shadows, a fire shining brightly through the ocean of darkness in Svalbard. Ilo's love and fleeting sense of fate seemed to be her only allies, yet Max couldn't help but fret over their sustainability. There were no promises of what things would be like once the event was over, and no guarantees that this connection would endure. There was no faith in a better life.

"Another underlying assumption in bioethical discussions is that cognitive enhancers will be utilized to pursue personal gains or to gain an edge over others," admitted Amos cautiously, "but on a societal scale, the cumulative effects of numerous minor individual enhancements could be significant. Even a small boost in overall intelligence could significantly reduce the number of intellectual disabilities and learning difficulties."

Max knew too well that such initial flames did not remain, and that beliefs of eternities are often wrapped in myths and lies. Soon enough, Ilo's warm and wet palm could become again too steady, too dry, only evoking love and trust lost again in the race of time.

"I do understand the fear and agitation created around such topics," advanced Amos. "But I urge those who are concerned to be able to discern what's purely medical research and advancement from speculative science fiction. The immediate goal of mind enhancement and brain-to-computer research isn't to drop imagery and stories into one's brain. It is, rather, to expand its possibilities to horizons that none of us can yet desire."

Promptly, a hand arose from the crowd.

"If we alter ourselves through cognitive enhancement technologies, even only for learning or creative capabilities, could we risk becoming less authentic and, consequently, diminish the value that authenticity brings to our lives?"

Amos answered with a playful, still naughty smile: "Well, let me return the question. What is the 'true' self in this era?"

The crowd began to whisper.

"I'm not here to dismiss the previous presentations, criticisms, or the critical work that has been done. I simply want, by the end of this week, to remind everyone to distinguish between science fiction and storytelling and the genuine altruistic and humanitarian visions of medicine. Let's not remain confused. Let's not slow progress down."

***

In her room, seated in the chair, trying to finalize her thoughts and words for the report, Max was struggling to keep her focus. Sifting through her memories, she tried to piece together the week's events, but nothing had truly stuck with her. She could only hear the steady workings of the pipelines. All the images were blurring together: the colors of love and illusions, the lectures and small deceptions, the slides and quiet sighs.

As voices and mechanical symphonies intertwined, the building itself began to whisper melodies and languages that were too abstract for Max to gather. Glancing at her notebook, the white and blank page stared back.

The clock was ticking at her side.

She grabbed a pencil and shortly wrote down: "Once the appetite for the real is gone... it takes a miracle to bring it back."

16.

In the very early morning of the seventh day, Max was tossing and turning in her bed, lost in layers of comforter and sweat. In her somniferous battles, Max had learned to reposition her necklace slightly, just to ensure it didn't break under the pressure of movement.

Yet, this time, at the slight touch of her neck, she realized that the pendant was no longer there. In an automatic, almost forceful motion, Max yanked the switch of her bedside light and began to turn over the bed, comforter, and pillows.

Disoriented and wide awake, the quest soon ended: the necklace was nowhere to be found. Lying down again, Max tried to recall the events of the previous day, the discussions, the gestures.

Nothing came to her mind.

She grabbed her phone: 3:30 AM. There were only two possible options: to remain motionless, searching for a memory that wouldn't come back, or to turn the room upside down.

Max got up and began turning over her suitcase, sheets, and towels, closely scrutinizing every nook and cranny of the room as if a crime scene. In a jerk, between the comforter and the slats, her hand brushed the knife, leaving a slight cut on her index finger.

Suddenly, and as if announced by some unknown grace, the necklace found its way to a corner of the bed, pretentiously posed to taunt Max. At the sight of the object, Max felt relieved, but it did not last.

Observing the charm, Max noticed that the necklace was neither broken nor cracked, but was in perfect condition, closed and secured at the clasp.

There was no rational explanation that could account for how the object could have been removed from her neck, displaced, and closed again.

***

By the time the first lecture started, Max had passed over every possible scenario in her head, rendering all the feasible moments and ways that one object can open and close itself. Yet, there seemed to be no reasonable way that such a thing could happen.

Running late, after quickly grabbing breakfast at the buffet before sitting down in the last row, Max tried to make herself as small as possible, hoping that no one and nothing would approach her.

In the conference room, the temperature formed a halo of humidity around the crowd. Max, at this point more than sleep-deprived, could no longer discern the unfamiliar figure who was standing in the spotlights.

Only the voice stood out: "Whether contemplating the allure of Instagram filters, immersive augmented reality experiences, or the emergence of misunderstandings born in virtual spaces, technology daily and constantly shapes our perception and imagination."

All the pieces of information floated through the space.

The speech was just another thought drifting through Max's brain before exiting again.

With her eyes half open, Max noticed that she wasn't the only one who was softly cradling out. Amos and Elena, too, seemed to struggle to remain present, fighting against the urge to fall asleep. Her gaze wandered around the conference room.

A voice came her way from behind: "Oh damn... Do you think that they'll again talk about fucking Pokémon Go?"

Max did not need to turn to immediately recognize Jona's voice amongst the thickening songs of the pipes, which had now become soft, brown and white background noise.

"Virtuality has become an integral aspect of our daily lives," the speaker continued. "The juxtaposition of online interactions surpassing face-to-face conversations, the ubiquity of online gaming communities, and individuals dedicating themselves to pursuits like playing full-time all underscore the profound impact of virtual experiences on our existence."

"See. I told you," whispered Jona.

He bent over to Max, who seemed on the verge of passing out. Max stared at Jona's watch. 10:15 AM. Minutes had never moved so slowly, yet the days had flown by.

"What day are we?" whispered Max.

"Thursday,"

"And the date?"

"Second of February."

The second of February. One day before the end of the conference. A few hours before the first return of sunlight.

"Fucking Ghaner," Max thought while smiling at the void.

Her eyes shifted back to the presenter on the stage.

"For years, we have already been seamlessly merging virtual and physical worlds, embedding digital creatures into our real surroundings. These experiences, all together, partake in the making of what I call 'the phenomenology of augmented life'. However, a compelling question arises in the context of such experience: could fantasy and perception be united?"

Max looked at the only possibly functioning window in the lecture room. It was far away from her, yet in the smallest corner, she could see the dark sky slowly beginning to turn blue. She could see the shimmering hints that could not yet be called a sunrise.

"The emergence of what would be called 'digital daydreaming', for example, encapsulates a specific type of mental wandering that occurs within the context of digital technology. This phenomenon refers to getting lost in one's thoughts or imagination while engaging with digital devices. This prominence brings forth myriad issues, such as the impact of filters on self-perception, the formation of echo chambers, the proliferation of fake news distorting realities, or the exacerbation of body dysphoria."

As the world surrounding the science center awakened, the crowd faded out. Everything around Max was caught in a strange twilight, suspended between night and day, between reality and illusion.

The sunlight made buds sprout from the corner of the room, slowly blossoming into trees that reached toward the ceiling. The empty chairs around her morphed too, disintegrating gradually, leaving behind the lifeless forms of the audience sprawled on the floor. It was as if they were being prepared for a greater purpose, their essence ready to nourish the roots of nature's insatiable hunger.

"As we overlay virtual content onto our sensory perception, the line between reality and digital fabrication blurs increasingly," the speaker continued, his voice deepening with seriousness. "This raises concerns about the trustworthiness of information and challenges our capacity to discern between genuine and manipulated experiences. There, the question 'Have you seen what I've seen? Have you read what I've shared?' takes on a new dimension, emphasizing the complex dynamics of sharing and validating experiences in the augmented realm."

As the speech came to its end, Bill applauded vigorously before searching for a curious hand or a wandering eye.

No one was moving. The only sound came from the loud breathing of the pipes.

In the desert of this awkward moment, Klara raised her hand, and to Bill's surprise, appeared straight next to him to grab the microphone: "I'm sorry," she said, "but the relationship between democracy and digital divergence is a little... elusive. Could you elaborate, perhaps?"

"Certainly," answered the speaker. "My argument is that such a phenomenon could create a divide between those who embrace augmented tools and those who don't, similar to the epistemological problem of other minds, where understanding others' experiences is the central issue. This divergence may diminish our ability to empathize with diverse viewpoints."

Klara nodded, whispering a brief "Thanks," before returning to her seat.

Promptly, without introducing herself, another participant raised her hand, slowly moving toward the microphone before spitting out a few words.

"I'm sorry, but in such a world, how do you know what you should believe and shouldn't trust?"

The speaker remained quiet. After inflexing his finger next to his mouth a few times, he reached for the microphone and claimed, while staring directly at Max: "You pay very close attention to your body and your daily senses. The body does not know how to lie to you. Pay very little attention to your mind. It is lying to you. All the time."

***

The discussions at the dinner table were heating up.

"I'm sorry," Amos interjected, "But how should we differentiate between enhancement technologies in your view? Should we be concerned about smart home devices? Is my Apple Watch a threat? What exactly are you getting at?"

"Oh, come on," Jona replied, with a clearly frustrated tone.

"You know exactly what I'm talking about. It's not about trivial home devices or trackable wearables. I'm talking about technologies that are too close to our skin, too near our brains, perhaps as permissive parts of our habits, in our dependence, which directly challenge the boundaries of our minds."

The other guests were waiting for Amos to bounce back, but instead, he stopped the discussion: "That's enough. Let's discuss this privately."

Max, sweating and barely breathing, inched from her dinner chair toward the bathroom.

There, she encountered Bill, who was also looking for ways to cool down.

The man who was initially standing strong, once wearing his proud and confident smile while speaking about the possible outcomes of critical research, was now standing still, faded, with a weary gleam in his eyes.

His gaze had changed, as if he did not need to pretend anymore, as if his mission had been terminated.

Max stood beside him in silence, waiting for him to step aside. He leered at her for an instant and smiled melancholically.

"Max, you seem sick... You should rest."

"I will," sighed Max.

"What have you been up to, really? It's not like there's any marathon to run here."

"I'm thinking about the report," retorted Max. "That's what's been on my mind."

"Ah, but don't worry about that. It's more of a... formality," answered Bill while patting Max on the back.

Max looked at Bill in confusion.

He glanced back, amused: "You did not seriously think that this event could change anything, right?"

Max splashed ice-cold water into her face.

As it awakened her senses, bringing her back to consciousness, she realized that Astrid had been nowhere to be found all day and night. When Bill walked out, she turned around and probed him about it.

He softly replied that she had left for personal reasons and that he couldn't provide any details.

Max was taken aback. Astrid would not have done such a thing without notifying anyone, nor presenting her research, nor following through on her initial promises. Yet, no one else seemed to question her departure. Her name had already been overshadowed by another online lecture. She was already a forgotten figure, part of a disappearing archive.

17.

Once dinner was over, Max felt the urge to go look for Ilo.

Making her way through the dimly lit space, she moved quietly toward the other side of the decaying building's carcass. In the shadows of the lounge corner, she spotted two figures who resembled Klara and Elena, entwined in a soft embrace, their figures merging into the darkness that surrounded them.

Unsure of the scene that was playing out, Max started to tiptoe, hoping that nobody else would notice her odyssey. But it was too late; in the blink of an eye, Elena turned around and smiled at Max.

Staring back at them, Max froze, trapped in an arena where she had neither a weapon to defend herself nor words to protect her.

While holding Klara's thigh, Elena whispered: "You see, Max... It's not that hard."

Max pretended not to hear Elena's words and continued walking, programmed for just one task.

After three knocks, Ilo opened the door. Max saw in her face the realization that this moment might be their last.

Max ghosted into the room and lay down on the couch. Ilo joined her.

They were both muted by the intensity and awkwardness that goodbye implies.

In a possible and alternative future, Max would have stayed with Ilo; they would have grown together, Max would have had to get used to Ilo's indifference, get used to the change in her gaze, get used to the shift in tone and silence, and the space of that empty fate.

In another timeline, they would have fought about what they already knew too well.

But Max had chosen her path. Neither of them would ever know. Staring at the ceiling, Max made peace with not knowing where things began or ended and which moments were lived or merely imagined. Perhaps it was monstrous to live that way. Perhaps it was less painful than watching love unravel before her eyes.

"What now?" Ilo asked.

Max turned around, gazing into Ilo's eyes. Her aura carried a spark, the tangible proof of change, the benefit of the doubt. The other timeline in which she was to leave Svalbard along Ilo's side, the one in which they chose the world, the choice of pain and sorrow, but at least, the choice of life.

"I have no idea," said Max.

Max lay there in silence, watching Ilo as she began to draw something on a piece of paper. She observed Ilo's delicate strokes as she outlined the contours of Svalbard, bathed in the warm hues of the newborn lights. Ilo's confidence in the sun's inevitable return radiated through her pencil onto the paper, capturing the soft strobe of light with each careful line.

Max found herself entranced by the drawing as if peering into a world filled with possibilities, a tomorrow where everything might just work out. Yet, as she gazed at the vibrant landscape, she couldn't picture herself within it.

"You want to add something to it?" Ilo asked.

Max leaned closer, her heart heavy with uncertainty. What, if anything, could she contribute to this vision of hope?

With a deep breath, she grabbed a pen, feeling its coolness in her hand.

With determination, she held the paper steadily and began to draw a path, a winding line that started at the Science Center and ventured into the unknown.

***

That night, resting in Ilo's arms felt like a mirage. Although they did not know what the future held, a sense of peace surrounded them, enabling them to ease into sleep. In that moment, while she felt her awareness slowly fading, Max wished to never wake up again and to remain at Ilo's side forever.

Falling into Morpheus's arms, Max began to notice the pattern.

A room full of darkness. A door that suddenly opened. The strange figure appeared, its back illuminated by the light from outside. The incapacity of moving away and the muteness imposed by the event's gravity.

As always, she was paralyzed, unable to cry out. Then, abruptly, a fracture pierced the room, shattering the deliberate darkness that was imposed. Entering through the door, the strange figure materialized, yet leaving Max unsure of its identity. She abruptly leaped up from the couch in an attempt to rouse Ilo, who remained undisturbed.

The figure, initially mistaken for Amos, appeared fragile and feminine, endlessly changing in shape. Transforming from Elena's figure into Klara's. The closer it got, the more it did not look like any particular individual, but rather as a monstrous mixture of all the individuals and guests she had met in Svalbard.

The familiar sleep paralysis disabled her completely. As the figure drew nearer, she felt a suffocating weight and tried to shout the words that were trapped in her throat.

Despite her efforts to flee, the insubstantial figure merged into Ilo.

Aware of her delirium, Max attempted to bang her head against the wall to awaken herself, but her body remained unresponsive. Ilo's figure, now fully possessed by it, approached Max.

Max found herself paralyzed, unable to escape the unsettling tableau.

Ilo only drew nearer, holding Max's knife and pointing it at her.

When Max finally woke up, tears and sweat had already dried on her face.

Ilo was asleep next to her, undisturbed and impartial. With a mix of gratitude and lingering despair, Max realized what had just transpired.

It was, once again, just a bad dream.

Glancing at the clock, she noted that a few hours had passed. Max could fall asleep again, but she was scared of what she would experience. Faced with the impossibility of believing in change, unable to say goodbye, and scared of her thoughts, Max knew that for her, only one option remained.

She stared at the wall for an hour before deciding to get up.

Still perspiring from her nightmare, Max dressed silently, her movements shrouded in quietness as she observed Ilo's serene, tranquil face.

Woken up by Max's movements, Ilo asked: "Where are you going?"

"I'll be back."

Ilo smiled gently before closing her eyes again.

Max looked again at Ilo's serene face. Why wasn't she stopping her? Perhaps, Max thought, Ilo knew what was about to happen. From the moment she first opened the door, leaving every password to be seen and not hidden, to the tales she had been telling Max about dying or being alive. From the gestures to the dreams, the pieces of the puzzle clicked in Max's mind.

Ilo could not do anything for her.

She existed as a reminder of what she had dreamed to be, to do, and still, in all possible ways, could not reach out. She would not heal her; she could not save her. Max dried her last tears, and in a perfect choreography of stealth and silence, she walked slowly down the long corridor.

As she reached her room, she dressed up for a hike.

***

Slipping into her clothes, Max mulled over all the things she had not yet finished and the people she had not yet said goodbye to. A part of her was bitter, and many things felt unfinished, but she had tried to do her part. She recalled how, excited and delighted, she once jumped out of her chair and signed the NDA contract without reading a line.

Before leaving Vienna, she had kept her trip to herself, not mentioning it to anyone. She walked around promising to hand in her next papers on time, saluting strangers whose names she never remembered.

She recalled how, when she left the main building, her co-worker Meli seized the opportunity to ask one more time: “Do you have some free time tonight?”

“What about... in the next two weeks?” Max had proposed, scrambling for the right words, attempting to hide her lie.

Somehow, she had known there would be no next week, no next times.

There was a new chapter to open, and Max was clueless about what to fill it with. She guessed that Ghaner and Elena would quickly notice her absence. She assumed that it would cast her as an unprofessional and unreliable figure in this theater of the absurd, but at this point, she couldn’t care less.

She never wanted to return.

As she left the room, Max saw a tiny, shiny object in the corner of her sight. It was the necklace she had forgotten to put on. Looking at the object, a tear dropped down her cheek. Max grabbed the charm and put it in her pocket astutely. She scribbled on the first piece of paper she found: “Every time I try, I can hear my wounds whispering: Who will you fool this time?”

Max did not sign it but drew the shape of the necklace’s symbol on the paper’s opposite side. She retrieved the knife from under the bed, and despite being somewhat underdressed for the cold outside, she promptly fled the bedroom, heading toward the airlock.

But when Max stepped out of the room, a strange, mechanical hum seemed to emanate from the heat-forecasting area. Wary, Max shifted direction toward the building's far end.

From a distance, she recognized the figure of one of the reporters. The movements were frantic, as if overwriting settings and seizing control of the system, as if hijacking it.

"Heat rage..." murmured Max, terrified to realize that perhaps the building wasn't malfunctioning, per se, but defective by design.

Navigating the long, overheated corridors, thoughts of destruction swirled through Max's mind. Pipes breaking, cameras shattering, crowds shouting, the weight of responsibility and blame no longer uncertain.

Max ran towards the exit, the password playing on repeat in her mind.

As she finally arrived at the airlock, Max took no gloves, no gun.

She quickly typed down the numbers she had memorized.

Opening the door, Max noticed the dawn blue light seeping through the dusk. Sick of her face and her skin in the ocean of darkness, where only a tint of light seemed to come in, she made her way outside.

Seized by the icy chill that stole her breath every time, Max continued walking. With the determination she knew from the treadmill, though still shrouded in doubt, she ventured into the timid daylight.

It began to illuminate the land.

When Max turned around, the young blue light infused the building and the surroundings of Svalbard with a fresh vibrancy. The snow seemed to disappear into the sky, making the structure appear as if it were floating, almost hovering into the heavens.

At that moment, the weight of her worries about the future faded away. She spun around, eager to continue. There was nothing in the world, nothing within herself, nothing externally, except the vast white landscape, that knew what might unfold next.

No one desired her presence, not the world, not the state, not even herself. Her steps breaking the snow's surface, heading toward the edge of the landscape, a knife in one hand, the bud in another one, Max softly repeated to herself the final lines of Karyn's Boye poem:

Then, at the point of agony and when all is beyond help,
The tree's buds burst as if in jubilation,
then, when fear no longer exists,
the branch's drops tumble in a shimmer,
forgetting that they were afraid of the new,
forgetting that they were fearful of the journey –
feeling for a second their greatest security,
resting in the trust

that creates the world.

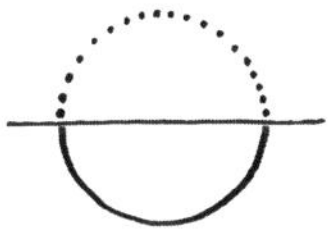

Thanks to Juli Frodermann and Hyun Vin Kaspers for helping me bring this building to life.

Thanks to people who loved me and supported me throughout the writing process, specifically Aman Cavalli, Liu Wei-Chen, Mira Samonig, Jonas Morgenthaler, Sam Fuentes, Lucia Ugena, Carmen Lael Hines and Florian Sigl.

Thanks to Adriana Lasheras, Alisa Petrosova, Sophie Publig, Max Mulhollandlicht, and Jean Renaud Billuart for reading my drafts.

Thanks to Lies Kelder for editing this text, Ryder Books for design and technical support, the Mondriaan Fund, Stichting de Zaaier, and Set Margins for helping me bring this book to life.

Thanks to Geert Lovink and my family for always believing in me and pushing me to write.

Set Margins' #89

The Heat of Others
By Morgane Billuart

Editor: Lies Kelder
Graphic design: Jordi de Vetten, Ryder Books
Advisor(s): Set Margins, Geert Lovink
Printer: PBTisk
Fonts: JL Limpet Granite & Bookmania

First edition, 2026
ISBN: 9789083657530
www.setmargins.press

Made possible thanks to the generous support of the Mondriaan Fund and Stichting de Zaaier.

mondriaan fund

STICHTING DE ZAAIER